Vermin

Enfield & Wizenty
(an imprint of Great Plains Publications)
1173 Wolseley Avenue
Winnipeg, MB R3G 1H1
www.greatplains.mb.ca

Great Plains Publications gratefully acknowledges the financial support
provided for its publishing program by the Government of Canada through
the Canada Book Fund; the Canada Council for the Arts; the Province of
Manitoba through the Book Publishing Tax Credit and the Book Publisher
Marketing Assistance Program; and the Manitoba Arts Council.

Design & Typography by Relish New Brand Experience
Printed in Canada by Friesens

LIBRARY AND ARCHIVES CANADA CATALOGUING IN PUBLICATION

Title: Vermin / Lori Hahnel.
Names: Hahnel, Lori, author.
Description: Short stories.
Identifiers: Canadiana (print) 20200278053 | Canadiana (ebook) 2020027810X |
    ISBN 9781773370460 (softcover) | ISBN 9781773370477 (ebook)
Classification: LCC PS8615.A365 V47 2020 | DDC C813/.6—dc23

ENVIRONMENTAL BENEFITS STATEMENT

Great Plains Publications saved the following
resources by printing the pages of this book on
chlorine free paper made with 100% post-consumer
waste.

TREES	WATER	ENERGY	SOLID WASTE	GREENHOUSE GASES
5	370	2	16	2,020
FULLY GROWN	GALLONS	MILLION BTUs	POUNDS	POUNDS

Environmental impact estimates were made using the Environmental Paper Network
Paper Calculator 4.0. For more information visit www.papercalculator.org.

Canadä

FSC
www.fsc.org
MIX
Paper from
responsible sources
FSC® C016245

VERMIN

STORIES

LORI HAHNEL

ENFIELD
&WIZENTY

I am still of the opinion that only two topics can be of the least interest to a serious and studious mood—sex and the dead.

—WILLIAM BUTLER YEATS

To Diane Girard,
Friend, fellow writer, fellow music lover,
confidant, and co-birthdayist

DOMINION

Though lovers be lost love shall not;
And death shall have no dominion.
—DYLAN THOMAS

July 1917

I open my eyes, and instead of my flowered bedroom walls, I see white all around me. For a second I am disoriented, afraid. I read the tag above my head: 'Abercrombie & Fitch Outfitters, New York.' Then my fog clears, and it comes to me: this is Tom's new tent. Completely waterproof, he said. I see beads of condensation on the other side of the heavy silk. He warned me not to touch the walls or water would wick through. But I can't resist: my finger comes away damp, and the drops jiggle and slide down the outside.

The sun is not completely up yet and already my upper lip and the nape of my neck are moist. Another muggy day. Last night, getting into the lake was all there was for it, never mind the leeches. Between the heat and the mosquitoes and the black flies, it was all we could do. I blush a little to think of it, but at the same time the memory is very pleasurable. The sound of Tom chopping wood outside breaks my reverie. Much as I would like to linger here a little longer and think of yesterday, another whole day is before us. The rest of our lives is before us. I try to forget the heat as I pull on my camisole, shirtwaist, drawers, stockings, petticoat and skirt. My boots are outside, and I unfasten the ties at the front of the tent. He stands in front of the fire he has started and smiles.

"Good morning," he says. He's dressed, has already combed his shock of dark hair.

"Good morning."

"Coffee?"

"Yes, please."

. . .

The hot and sleepy Sunday morning before, I discreetly wiped perspiration from my lip and hairline with the back of my glove as Father and Mother and I listened to Reverend MacAllister's sermon. "God gave man Dominion over the fish of the sea and the fowl of the air," he said. "Over the *cattle,* and over all the earth. He gave man Dominion over his helpmate, woman. God gave man Dominion over all of Nature, that he might subjugate it, that he might profit from it. That he might order nature as he sees fit, that he might control it."

I looked at my parents' blank faces. No face around us had any expression save possibly boredom. A few of the ladies fanned themselves. Mary Carlson's baby began to fuss and squall and she whisked him outside. I wondered if I were was the only one listening to the sermon. I am certain that I was the only one questioning it.

Later, as I tended the garden, I thought about the Reverend's words again, about man subjugating nature. It's certainly happened here with the forests, even in Algonquin Park, being logged at a great rate. Mother's garden is nature subjugated on a smaller scale. First, I pulled up all the weeds, the wild plants that have no business in the garden. Then I filled the watering can with rainwater collected in the barrel and watered the rows of onions, potatoes and carrots we'll store in the cellar, and the beets, scarlet runner beans and peas that Mother and I will can in the fall. Even the petunias Mother has planted in front of the just-whitewashed verandah are under strict control. They are planted in neat rows, exactly twelve inches apart, dead-headed and trimmed regularly. Although these plants are grown simply for pleasure, they are tamed and domesticated by man, cross-pollinated over and over quite purposefully to obtain the precise colour and scent desired. Still, I notice that the petunias' perfumed velvet trumpets, a shockingly sensual fuchsia with a deeper, private purple within, still tremble with the slightest breeze. They haven't bred that out of them yet.

I know just how Tom would paint them.

. . .

This year we had fireworks on the lake on Dominion Day. On July 2nd, actually—July 1 was a Sunday. They scared poor Tige, our black and tan collie, so much that he shot under the front porch when they started and didn't come out for almost an hour. Mr. Fraser, the big raw-boned man from the Mowat Lodge, set them off on the end of the dock and everyone gathered to watch. I hadn't seen Tom all day, but he came up behind me in the crowd and put his arm around my shoulders just as the last scarlet Roman candle went off, reflecting on the calm surface of Canoe Lake.

"Friday?" he whispered in my ear.

I nodded, looked around to see if anyone was listening.

"You're sure?"

"Yes."

He gave me a squeeze in answer just as Father came up. "Evening, Tom."

"Evening, sir," Tom replied, dropping his arm.

"Winnie, it's time to come home now."

"Yes, Father. Goodnight, Tom."

Father and I started back to our cottage. He mopped his glistening forehead with a handkerchief Mother had embroidered with his initials. Although it was almost midnight, the heat was still awful, oppressive.

"When is he going to get serious?"

I had no answer to that. None that would have satisfied him, anyway. "I do love him, Father."

Father never had much use for Tom, and he'd said as much to me and Mother many times. On the other hand, I was thirty-two now. No one had yet used the word 'spinster', but it loomed. "I know you do, Miss. But does he feel the same way? Is he ready to settle down?"

"It may be that he is," I said. Father just sighed and shook his head.

. . .

The next morning, as I hung the washing I'd just finished out on the line and batted away humming mosquitoes, I thought about Father's words. He didn't understand that Tom and I are different—not from each other, but from other people. We're different in the same way. I've always been on the outside somehow, never even realized until I met him that someone else could be like me. Tom is himself above all else. He lives the way he sees fit, does the work he must do. Listens to the voice inside that tells him what his life must be. And the more I think of it, the more I understand that that's the way I am, too. To live any other way seems wrong to me. Father could never understand that. Most people around here don't. I've heard the talk. He is lazy. He is irresolute. He will never settle down. Some have even implied he's a coward because he's not overseas fighting.

But he's nearly forty. They wouldn't need him to fight, would they, unless they become desperate for men?

A soft, steady chirp nearby distracted me. On the top spire of the Jack pine behind our cottage sat a red-headed finch, singing alone. I remembered reading that although these finches were introduced to Canada as house pets, there was now a sizeable wild population. They must have escaped, or perhaps people let them go. Either way, they're free now.

After hanging up the laundry I took a few moments to check over the contents of my travelling bag. It's large, made of leather with brass mountings. Besides some everyday clothes, most of the things inside it were from my hope chest at home: a cedar blanket box that has sat at the foot of my bed as long as I can remember. Inside, folded in tissue paper, was my trousseau: Mother's cream silk satin and lace wedding gown and veil. A fine bridal nightgown, tucked and embroidered white silk, light and delicate as a whisper. A soutache embroidered ecru linen travelling suit Aunt Esther made for me. The Bible Mother and Father presented me with at my confirmation. A heather grey angora shawl. A straw braid hat with a wide blue taffeta ribbon and grey ostrich plumes. My own copy of *Mrs. Beeton's Book of Household Management*. I have sometimes looked at Mother's copy, but it intimidates me. A thousand pages. So much that a woman is expected to know and do and take care of. Is this what we were put here for, to toil and organize, clean, order, compile? Subjugate? When I was packing, I opened my copy at a random place and read:

> Of all those acquirements, which more particularly belong to the feminine character, there are none which take a higher rank, in our estimation, than such as enter into a knowledge of household duties; for on these are perpetually dependent the happiness, comfort, and well-being of a family.

I closed the book. Back into the box with Mrs. Beeton.

Before we left for Canoe Lake this time, I slipped the travelling suit, a corset, the nightgown, the hat and the shawl into the leather bag, and when we arrived at the cottage, stowed it under my bed.

"Winnie," called Mother from outside. "Are you here? I need your help."

"Coming, Mother."

I closed the bag, put it back under the bed and went to find Mother.

. . .

Father's job with the Huntsville Lumber Company allowed him to buy the cottage on Canoe Lake. "Now we'll be able to relax," he'd said. I'm not sure how much we're relaxing. It seems to me there is as much work to do at the cottage—cooking, cleaning, household management—as there is at home, but it is nice to get away sometimes. And Algonquin Park is beautiful.

The Wednesday after Dominion Day Father received a wire saying he was needed to settle an urgent matter at the mill back in Huntsville. He thought it shouldn't take more than a day or two, after which he and Mother would come back to the cottage and finish his vacation. They were to take the train into Huntsville Friday and return the next Tuesday and agreed that I should stay on at the cottage. The timing was quite providential.

Late Friday afternoon Mr. Fraser's 'hearse', as his wagon was called, arrived to take them to the train station.

"We'll see you in a few days, Winnie. Don't forget about the garden while we're gone," Mother said as they climbed into the wagon.

"I won't forget. Have a safe journey. Goodbye."

I waved and watched until I could no longer see the wagon and its plume of dust. Then I went to the garden directly and gave everything a thorough soaking. I pulled the weeds, trimmed and deadheaded. Before long I became aware of a strange feeling—a tightening in my stomach. I thought at first, I might be hungry. Then I thought it might have been that same sick feeling I'd had in the mornings until a couple of weeks previous. But this was something else. Excitement, fear, dread—it seemed to be a mixture of all these things.

Inside the cottage, I made sandwiches to take along, steeled myself. This was not the time for second thoughts. We knew that our parents would be beside themselves when they discovered that we had to get married. So we talked it over and agreed that going away was a good idea. Tom had been planning to go out West and paint in the summer anyway; his friend Alex Jackson had sketched in Mount Robson Park in British Columbia a couple of years earlier, and Tom had been set on going to the Rockies ever since. We would canoe to Parry Sound, where we weren't so well-known, catch a train to Toronto and from there take the Canadian Northern to the West. Tom had a cousin in Calgary who was a minister, and he was sure he'd be able to marry us without too much trouble.

This was finally it. After thirty-two years of living in the same town with the same people (all of whom know all of each other's business all the time and pretend they don't), my life was on a new course. Tom and I would have a new life in the West, away from the gossip, the judgement, the small-mindedness that have confined me all my life. I caught a glimpse of myself in the mirror on my dresser as I reached under the bed for my travelling bag and couldn't help smiling. What a lucky woman, I thought.

I found a piece of writing paper and an envelope and sat down to write Mother and Father a note. I hadn't been going to but changed my mind at the last moment. I did not wish to worry them or hurt them more than I had to.

Dear Mother and Father:

    Tom and I are going away to be married. I am sorry to have to tell you this way, but this is what I must do now. I will write you once we are settled in our new home and explain everything. Please don't worry about me.

    Ever your loving Winnie

I folded the note, put it in the envelope and left it on the table. Then I picked up my bag. Dusk was just beginning to fall as I left to meet Tom.

. . .

We decide that there is no rush for us to get to Parry Sound—after all, Mother and Father won't be returning until Tuesday. And while I imagine they're in for a big shock, I am an adult. They cannot stop us; nothing can stop what has already begun. We came a little distance from Canoe Lake the first night, then set up camp. Saturday, we fish, Tom does some sketching. We make love. And by night we haven't gone much further. But the time we have spent together the last couple of days is what I always hoped my life could be like. Surely this kind of living is what Nature intended for human beings. I can't ever remember being so happy.

After a dinner of trout, we sit together and watch the moon begin to rise through the silhouettes of trees. Tom's pipe keeps the mosquitoes away a little. We sip coffee, Tom's laced with rum, listen to the sonorous songs of frogs. He takes a long drag on his pipe and exhales a lazy plume of smoke.

"Winnie," he says. "I've been thinking. Fraser still owes me a good deal of money."

"From when he bought the canoes for the lodge?"

"Yes. And we'll need money in the next few months. I think before we go any further, I'll go back and ask him for it."

"Tonight?"

He nods. "It won't take me long. If I leave now, I can be back an hour or two after midnight. Then we should be able to get to Parry Sound tomorrow and be on our way to Toronto."

I am too tired to disagree with him, though I'd really rather not be here on the river alone. But he'll only be away a few hours, and he's right. We're going to need all the money we can get.

The canoe glides silently over the surface of the water as Tom heads back in the direction of Mowat Lodge. As he disappears from view, the feeling of dread I had when I left the cottage on Friday returns. I close the tent and settle into the sleeping bag, tell myself it's just nervousness at being left alone. Soon Tom will be back, and we'll be on our way.

I listen to the frogs, the gentle murmur of the water, begin to drift off. This is all happening for a reason. It's becoming clear to me now. I understand now why I had all those years of loneliness—because I had to wait for Tom. Together we can live the lives we were meant to. New lives in a new land. Soon I sleep.

. . .

I don't really begin to worry until noon. I had woken with the sun, around seven, and wondered where he was but thought he might have decided to sleep at the lodge instead of coming back in the dead of night. But the higher the sun climbs, the more uneasy I begin to feel. Where is he? We won't make it to Parry Sound in time for the train if he doesn't come soon. I busy myself packing things, taking the tent down, so that I'll be ready when he arrives. I feel stranded here, no canoe, no way of contacting him, not even really sure how far upriver I am.

As dusk begins to fall, I decide I must set up the tent again. I'm a little unsure how, but I did watch Tom do it, and before long I get it done. I have been able to calm myself in the last few hours. I trust him completely. Whatever the reason is for this delay I know it's a good one. Everything will be all right. I get in the tent and fall asleep quickly.

The next morning there is still no sign of him, and I feel panicky. I try to eat a little of the bread we have left but I'm not sure I'll be able to keep it down. Then I spot a canoe heading toward me. My heart jumps, but soon I see that it's not Tom's blue canoe. As it comes closer, I see that it's Mark Robinson, the park ranger.

"Winnie. I'm glad to see you," he says.

"Have you seen Tom?"

He grimaces, rubs the back of his neck. "I was hoping he'd be with you. They found his canoe this morning, turned over on Canoe Lake."

. . .

Eight long, wrenching, awful days go by. Mother and Father return to the cottage; I must tell them my whole story. Their reaction is beyond anger, beyond hurt. They are profoundly disappointed, simply seem shut down. They cannot accept what I have done. Meanwhile, my hopes sink more and more with each passing moment. Has the new life I thought I had found already become a long-ago dream? I look over and over at the handful of sketches Tom gave me, run my fingers over the brushstrokes, pray that he is just lost somewhere and on his way back to me.

Mother and Father and I sit silently on the front porch staring at the steel grey sky when Mark Robinson comes with the news that they have found Tom floating in the lake.

Mother's face sinks into her hands. Father can only meet my eyes for a moment. He turns his gaze from my sobbing, my raw, open emotion. He thanks Mark, takes my upper arm, and leads me into the cottage.

Father's voice is a dull, leaden knell. "Winifred. No one must ever hear a word of any of this. None of it. You and Mother will take a trip over the winter to visit relatives. After that we need never speak of it again."

He keeps talking, but I no longer understand what he's saying. I feel as though I am underwater. It might as well have been me on the bottom of that lake instead of Tom. For I have sunk even further than he had, at least in the eyes of the town and my parents. I want to answer, say something, but I cannot. And it's of no consequence: I am back in Father's house, back under his dominion, for good, now.

VERMIN

Jurgen Koch has to be the worst cook in the world. So you wonder why he owns a restaurant, and why he cooks in it. It's simple: he owns a restaurant because it was an easy business for him to buy in Tofino. When he came here on vacation in the 90s and did the West Coast Trail, he fell in love with Vancouver Island and spent the next ten years saving up so he could move here from Germany. And he does the cooking himself because he's a cheap son-of-a-bitch who won't pay a real cook. I'd love to tell my impatient customer this, but I can't. I love living in Tofino, too, and I don't want to lose this job. *Suck it up, sweetheart,* I think. *You don't look like you're starving to me.*

Actually, this guy scared the bejesus out of me when he first came in. He looks a lot like my ex-boyfriend Ray's Uncle Lloyd. Dead ringer for him. He spooked me enough that I wanted Dirk to serve his table, but of course Dirk was nowhere in sight. Probably out back having a cigarette, listening to that techno/dance stuff he loves on his iPod. I had to reason with myself: how could it be Lloyd? Lots of old men look like that— short, leathery-faced, truck logo baseball cap, faded jeans held up around his skinny ass with a giant belt buckle. Once I went over and took his order and heard his voice, I realized he wasn't Lloyd, couldn't be. What was I thinking?

"Becka!" Jurgen calls from the kitchen. He's so cheap he can't even spring for one of those counter bells to ring when he finally has an order up. I'll have to get him one for his birthday.

The pale, hard half hot dog bun Jurgen has toasted and smeared thinly with garlic butter rattles lonely and ungarnished on the oval plate as I set it in front of the man. Yes, this is what he's been waiting for all this time. He looks at me, about to say something, about to complain. I head him off at the pass.

"You ordered the garlic toast, didn't you?" I ask, flash a flirtatious smile, flick the ends of my long, dark hair over my tanned shoulders. He flushes a little, glances at his tired-looking wife. A girl my age probably hasn't smiled at this guy since he was my age.

"Uh, yeah," he says quickly. "Thanks."

Another satisfied customer. Another disaster averted by my exceptional public service skills. I'll have to talk to Jurgen about a raise. Ha.

. . .

One of the things I love most about this place is the ocean smell. Southern Alberta smells like cow shit and diesel and sour gas wells. The ocean smells of life, and death. Of rot and salt. I like to walk up and down Long Beach, feel the sand between my toes. Look for whatever's washed up today. Shells, crabs, dead seals or birds, tires, driftwood, bottles. You never know what you'll find, different stuff every day.

Dirk and I surf a lot. On the west coast of the Island we get some of the best waves anywhere, surfers come here from all over the world. He usually uses a board, but I prefer bodysurfing. I need to throw myself against the water, feel the impact of my body against the waves. Is surfing addictive? I don't know. I do know that sometimes I only feel alive out here.

. . .

Ray's Uncle Lloyd lived on the section of land the family owned near Turner Valley, in the rolling foothills south of Calgary. At one time the family ranched there, but by the time we moved there it was only Lloyd left. I wasn't ever sure what he did. The yard in front of his house was full of cars and trucks that he worked on some of the time. Mostly I just saw him sit on the porch and drink beer and watch the cars that went by once in a while. Over the years the family built different houses on the land and eventually abandoned them as they built new ones. Ray and I lived the oldest house, on the other side of the barn near Lloyd's house. Lloyd must have seen the people coming and going day and night. Ray didn't think his uncle had any idea what he did. I wasn't so sure.

"Becka," Lloyd said, and grasped my hand a little too firmly, a little too long when Ray introduced us. "That short for Rebecca?"

"Yes, it is," I said, smiled tightly. *No shit, Sherlock. And you can let go of my hand now.*

Lloyd didn't like Ray's dog, Junior. Junior scared the shit out of me the first time I saw him, too. He's a Rottweiler cross. Crossed with a moose, I think. He's black and tan, muscular, huge. Luckily Junior loved me from the second we met. He came and lay at my feet and I rubbed his tummy and that was it; he was devoted to me from then on. Followed me everywhere. I'd never had a dog before, had no idea how loyal they can be. It's kind of cool.

Ray decided we should move out to the family's land after a friend of his got busted in Calgary. Don't get the wrong idea about Ray. He didn't always sell dope, at least not full time. He impressed me when I first met him. He worked as a roofer, made good money. He talked about going back to school part time, picking up some courses, starting a business. I liked that he had a plan. But after he hurt his back on a job he put in a claim for compensation and waited and waited and when they did settle, he got almost nothing. Hey, a guy's got to live. Still, after a while I realized my boyfriend had become a dealer. I wasn't sure how I felt about that. He always said it was temporary. But he'd been doing it almost a year and I never noticed him looking for a job. Plus, once he started working at home, he let himself go. His construction worker's physique got all soft, he let his hair go all wild. And he got into some kind of freaky Fu Manchu thing with his moustache. The idea was to intimidate people, I guess. I just thought he looked like Lemmy from Motorhead. Eww. Worse, unless he was making a delivery, he hung around the place all the time. He started to remind me of Lloyd. Maybe a cross between Lloyd and Lemmy. Creepy.

"What happened to all your plans?" I asked him after a while. "You know, going to school, starting your own business, all that."

"Well, I kind of have my own business now, don't I?"

"Um, yeah. An illegal business."

"Aw, c'mon, Becka. Give me a break. You know it's just temporary."

"Is it? I don't see you looking into any courses or anything like that. Or looking for another job, even."

"Get off my back. Okay?"

As for me, I worked waiting tables evenings at a diner in Turner Valley. Got me out of the house, I guess. I would have rather done something else, but there wasn't much to pick from. Turner Valley's pretty small. And it was great experience for working at Jurgen's Tofino House, as it turns out.

. . .

Ray got up early one morning in June to go to Calgary to make a delivery to one of his better customers. I didn't feel like going with him since he had no air conditioning in his truck and we were in the middle of a stretch of hot weather then. The days were sultry, overcast; thunder rumbled in the rainy afternoons and evenings. I thought I'd get out early in the morning and take Junior for a walk while it was still reasonably cool. Besides, I didn't feel like hanging around with Ray's pothead friends.

When Junior and I went by Lloyd's place I saw him take something out from under the eaves of the old barn near his house and throw handfuls of it against the wall, hard. When I got closer, I could see it was birds. He scooped baby birds out of nests that lined the eaves and threw them against the wall of the barn. Dead baby birds lay all along the bottom of the wall where he'd already been, barn cats gorged themselves.

"What are you doing?" I asked.

"Sparrows. Vermin. I'm getting rid of them."

"You're throwing baby birds against a wall."

I watched him shoo the cats away, fill a shovel with birds, throw them into a big slough, swollen from the rains, at the bottom of a slope behind the barn. "They're filthy. Shit all over everything. Damage the crops."

"What crops? You're not growing anything."

He squinted at me for a minute. "I don't need vermin on my property."

Sparrows screeched as Junior and I walked away. Funny, I hadn't noticed them before and now the sound was deafening.

. . .

The sign outside Jurgen's Tofino House says, 'Best Fish and Chips on Vancouver Island.' Of course, every restaurant on the Island has a sign that says that. Some of them claim to have the best fish and chips in the world. Well, I wouldn't say we have the best fish and chips on the Island. If it was up to me the sign would say, 'The food probably won't kill you' or maybe, 'Lunch usually doesn't take more than two hours' or something like that. It also says, 'Specializing in West Coast Cuisine.' Jurgen's interpretation of West Coast cuisine is a little, shall we say, loose. He relies heavily on frozen and processed ingredients and tends to shy away from local stuff, because of the expense of course. Dirk, loyal son that he is, claims his dad's cooking has improved in the ten years he's been here. I shudder to think that what he does now is the result of ten years' work.

Dirk and I have an understanding. He helps me out if I have a customer who's a little too friendly or a little too aggressive. I help him out if he has trouble with English. Not that he needs it that often. He's only been over here about a year and he's got an accent for sure, but he speaks English well. I always think about how I'd do in German. Not well, I think.

I'd like to meet Dirk's mom someday. He must get his tall, slim, blond looks from her. Jurgen always looks a little like a walrus to me: pudgy, big handlebar moustache, not blond or red or brown but somewhere in between. It's one of those compensatory moustaches some guys grow when they're losing it on top. Dirk's mom's name is Petra. She's an artist, lives in Berlin, works in a gallery. She and Jurgen divorced long ago. I'm thinking it won't be long until Dirk takes off for Vancouver. Not that a gay man would have a problem living in Tofino, but I think a gay man living with Jurgen could have a problem. Which is why it's so convenient that we can hang out together. Jurgen thinks we're in love. It doesn't bother me, but maybe someday Jurgen will figure it out, and I don't want to be around for that.

. . .

I have to say it didn't really surprise me when Ray got busted. I wondered if someone had narked on him. A pissed off customer, maybe, or even Lloyd. I had a bad feeling about Ray's court date, didn't think it would go well for him, especially after he told me this wasn't his first offense.

"What?"

"Uh, yeah, I had a prior conviction about five years ago. I swear, though, I just had a bag for personal use. Just an ounce."

"Why didn't you tell me that before?

"I didn't think it was important until now."

My parents didn't ever like Ray. They'd have flipped if they'd known he was in jail for trafficking. I thought at first I'd tell them he was away, travelling. In Europe for three to five. Then again, the more I thought about it the more it seemed like that was my cue. The end, time to go. I decided I'd head out to Vancouver Island for a while; I'd always wanted to live by the sea.

So I bought a bus ticket. Ray's sister Julie, who lives in Turner Valley, agreed to come by that day to take me to the Greyhound station in Calgary. She was also taking Junior to stay with her, said she'd keep him until Ray got out of jail. As I finished packing, Lloyd came by.

It all seemed to happen so fast. I've thought about it thousands of times and after a certain point I'm not sure what happened, exactly. It was another hot, humid day and I took Junior out for a walk, our last walk, before it got too hot. Even before we got back to the house, black clouds rolled in, the temperature dropped a few degrees. There was a big storm on the way, you could feel it in the air. Just as we got in the house, big, cold raindrops started to fall, hard and fast. I was about to change my sweat-damp clothes when I saw Lloyd standing in the kitchen, grinning. His green plaid shirt was stained, a film of sweat and a two-day beard covered his leathery face.

"What are you doing here, Lloyd?"

He dangled a key in front of my face. "Lots of keys to this place around. I got a few."

"I didn't ask how you got in. I asked what you were doing here."

He just smiled. "You miss Ray?"

"Sure. But it's time for me to move on. I'm leaving."

"He should have been more careful. He shouldn't have been

selling drugs on the family farm. Guess he thought I didn't know, but I did."

"So you called the cops?"

"I'm not saying that. All's I'm saying is he should have watched his step. Now he's losing a pretty girl like you. The boy's always been a fool."

A flash of lighting illuminated the windows for a moment and the tearing roar came close behind. Lloyd ignored it, slowly made his way toward me.

"You need to go back to your place now," I said.

He kept coming closer. "You wouldn't make me go out in the storm, would you?"

He wrapped a hand around my forearm. The more I tried to pull away, the harder he hung on. Black grease stained all the creases in his hands and around and under his thick, yellow fingernails. I smelled his sweat, the alcohol on his breath, his grimy clothes.

"Junior," I called quietly. I immediately heard the click of his claws on the floor behind me. I looked into Lloyd's eyes for a second before I said, "Get him, Junior."

As soon as Junior growled and started to lunge, Lloyd was off like a greasy little rocket, out the front door and heading in the direction of the barn. I didn't think he could move that fast.

He wasn't fast enough for Junior, though. I watched out the front door as the dog caught up with him. Junior's jaws caught him by the back of his upper thigh, pulled him to the wet, slippery ground. Lloyd screamed, "Call him off! Call him off!" He screamed like a girl. I had no respect for that.

Lloyd screeched as he and Junior rolled down a slope, and then I couldn't see them anymore. I heard a splash, so I guess they got into the slough. I pictured Lloyd thrashing among the bloated corpses of baby birds. Then thunder drowned out any other sound for a while.

I started to wonder whether I should go outside and see what happened, when Junior appeared in the doorway, soaked to the skin and panting hard.

"Poor Junior! Poor baby. You're all wet. Let Becka dry you off." I got a towel and rubbed him down. I didn't see any scratches, or any blood on his fur. Which would have maybe washed off in the slough and the rain. There was something that looked like a long shred of cloth stuck in his teeth, green plaid. I pulled it out and threw it in the compost outside.

Junior had a drink of water and stretched out on the kitchen floor for a nap. Poor guy was exhausted. He'd had a busy morning. But when I woke him a little over an hour later so we could get into Julie's truck, he was fresh and ready to go. Dogs are funny like that.

. . .

The sea looks like the sky looks like the sea. Gulls screech as they circle overhead, screech as they divebomb the surf. I watch one dive in, dip, come out with a long shred of cloth stuck in its beak. But when I look again it's just a piece of kelp. Silly me.

Dirk and I are both working our usual 11 - 8 shifts today. We'll have to get moving pretty soon. But right now, we lie side by side, dry out in the sun on Long Beach, listen to the birds, warm up after surfing all morning. Today I feel like I could lie here forever. I don't want to go in to work, don't want to deal with Jurgen, deal with the customers.

"I'm thinking about moving to Vancouver, Becka," Dirk says.

"You'd love it there. It's a very cool city."

"You want to come with?"

"Maybe. When are you thinking of going?"

"Soon. Pretty soon."

"Can I think about it for a couple of days?"

"Of course. Take your time."

"Thanks. I'm not surprised, you know. You're from a big city. You must miss big city life."

"I do. Yes. What about you? Do you miss Alberta?"

I think about that for a minute before I answer him. "A little. Sometimes."

I don't miss much about Alberta, really. Except for maybe Junior.

ONLY KNOWN PHOTOGRAPH OF CHOPIN, 1849

I rush through the streets, late for an appointment, then suddenly stop dead. The snow-muffled sounds of people and carriages and horses on the rue Mazarine stop, too; I only hear blood pound in my ears. Frédéric. There he is, in a photograph displayed in the window of Bisson Fils, Photographes. I stare, try to catch my breath, feel as shocked as if he stood before me in the flesh. This must be the portrait he'd written me about, taken only weeks before he died. He complained about the neck clamp they'd used to keep him still during the exposure, about how uncomfortable and unwell he felt sitting there, about how he thought these young men and their machine could never do him justice the way Delacroix had in his famous painting. But everyone in Paris was having them done, he said, and he had to keep current.

The whole idea of these photographs still amazes me; I can stand here and look at Frédéric over a year after his death. He looks bewildered, suspicious, mistrustful. Perhaps of the photographers, perhaps of the future. The neuralgia he spoke of has swollen his face in the portrait. You can see how ill he has been by the way he looks lost in his cravat, by the way he swims in the overcoat he wears over his waistcoat. He wore that same overcoat, I remember, one November evening when a group of us got into a phaeton to go see Liszt at the Paris Opera House. By the gaslight I noticed a snowflake on his collar, and another, and another, small, perfect, crystals. They melted as they touched my cape and Schumann's coat, but they just piled up on Frédéric. Some fancy struck me that he must be colder than the rest of us, that he must lack some heat we had at our cores. How silly of me.

That same night Schumann told me, "Constantia. He will give you anything except himself." That, I already knew to be true.

. . .

A winter night, Berlin. Outside snow falls, the clouds are purple and heavy with snow. Inside the room is dark, except for the flicker of the firelight. One of us should really tend to it before it goes out. Music filled the first part of the evening, then food and wine and conversation. Now we only hear pops and crackles as the fire dies, and the sound of our breath. He has pulled the pins from my hair and it falls around my bare shoulders, his long fingers explore my stays, looking for buttons, clasps, closures. His breath is hot along my collarbone, my neck, my ear. He eases me onto my back on the eiderdown, and I shudder a little, feeling his weight on top of me as my hands roam across his back. The rhythm of our bodies becomes urgent, insistent.

It is a long time before we realize the fire has gone out.

. . .

When Frédéric wrote me about having the photograph taken I was a little surprised. Once I was in Paris to play Dorabella in Mozart's *Così fan Tutte* (I looked Frédéric dead in the eye during my aria "È amore un ladroncello." Love *is* a little thief). After the performance we all had dinner at Madame Sand's, and I remember a conversation about photographs.

"Ridiculous! A parlour trick," Frédéric had said. "These blurry little grey scraps of paper will never replace the art of portraiture."

Madame Sand laughed and lit a cigar. "I suppose you think gaslights will never replace candles. And locomotives will never replace horses. But this is the Age of Progress, my dear. Look at what science has achieved in our time."

"Amazing things," said Prince Radziwill from the end of the long, intricately carved dining table. "I hear a man here in Paris is at work on a machine that will record sound. Imagine that, Frédéric. You would never have to appear in a drafty concert hall again."

"That idea has some appeal for me," Frédéric admitted. "But how quickly the world changes! Women smoking cigars—"

Madame Sand interrupted. "And writing novels, don't forget."

"Yes, and writing novels. All these things our grandfathers never had to think about. Streets lit with gas. Machines to take us from one place to another, machines to record images, machines to record sounds. Where will it end? Do these inventions make life easier? Or just faster?"

"Perhaps they will make life better," the prince suggested. "Medicine discovers cures for diseases now. Imagine a world without cholera."

"Yes. Or tuberculosis," said Frédéric. "That would be something."

. . .

Frédéric knew he was dying for a long time, that the tuberculosis that had taken his sister Emilia at age fourteen, and his father just a few years before, would take him, too. He insisted that after his death his heart be cut out and sent to Warsaw.

This was not so much a matter of sentiment as sheer terror on his part, the terror of being buried alive. As a young man he had witnessed the cholera epidemic in Vienna. He wrote to me:

Dearest Constantia:

Pray for me, that I make it out of Vienna alive. All around here is death: the air is heavy with the smell of rotten flesh, with smoke from the victims' houses, which they burn to the ground. They say that in the chaos people are being buried alive! I will make my way to Bavaria in the next few days, though I'm sure the cholera will be there before long, too.

Later the outbreak followed him to Paris. Two thousand Parisians died every day, the coffin makers could not keep up. Madame Sand wrote of bodies stuffed into old sacks and stacked into carts. Worse, when the starving survivors rioted, the National Guard was called out. More blood. The morgue overflowed, heads stacked in its windows, blood oozed out from under its doors and flowed into the Seine, already full of floating, bloated corpses. Who would think that someone as sickly, as delicate as Frédéric could live through that kind of horror? Yet he did. Like his music, he was a man of counterpoints, contrasts, contradictions.

. . .

An evening in Prague, after a performance. I cannot sleep, try to read a novel by Mr. Dickens. I read a paragraph, perhaps a page and then I have to set the book down as an image jolts unbidden into my mind: his hand moves slowly over my waist, my hips, stops mid-thigh. I read a few more lines and feel his breath behind my ear, his lips brush my neck, my shoulders. It's no use. I cannot sleep, I cannot read, I cannot stop thinking of our last night together, in Paris.

In the carriage on the way to his rooms he touched a finger to a crystal of the lavaliere that circled my throat and spilled onto my collarbone. He rolled it gently back and forth on my skin, never took his eyes from mine.

"This is beautiful," he whispered. As he kissed me his fingers slid up along my jawbone, back down my neck.

I put down Mr. Dickens, sink my face into my hands. My heart and my body scream that I must be near him. My mind is not so sure. I do know this: I believe that we are on this earth but once, and I believe that our time here is something like a snowflake's: beautiful, intricate, brief. And if everything within me tells me to be with him, can I really spend what little time I have in resistance?

Of course, it's not that simple. Nothing is that simple.

. . .

I don't think that Frédéric ever really understood the way I felt about him. Sometimes I'm not even so sure I did. First love, the man I never got over. Perhaps. I did get over him romantically. But he remained in my heart as conundrum, thorn in my side. And muse: the thought of him powered many of my aria performances. More, I thought of him as an admired artist, and beloved friend, though he might never believe that. At any given time my feelings for him seemed to shift like the light in a kaleidoscope.

When we were young, he sometimes called me 'Constanze', after Mozart's long-suffering wife. Close enough to Constantia, I supposed. He said in those days that he adored me. I am sure he did, in a way. But when we grew older, I realized that he would never be mine, he would never belong to anyone, not even Madame Sand. I only had to think of the power that went into his performances to know where his heart was. He had terrible, almost disabling stage fright: for days before a public appearance he would be irritable, jumpy, off his food. Somehow, he was able to channel that energy into his performances when he finally got onstage, and audiences responded. Not in the way they responded to Liszt. Women shrieked and kicked each other to get near Liszt. Frédéric's effect was quieter, more genteel. And unlike Liszt, who took advantage whenever he could, Frédéric loved the idea that women in the audience were charmed by him, but that was as far as it went. Perhaps that sums up Frédéric's feelings about women.

I remember a performance when he played the prelude that has come to be known as "Raindrop." The piece begins like a spring morning; beautiful, lively. Ornate and delicate as dew on a spider's web, a crystal chandelier, Madame Sand's necklace, sparkling when caught by a stage light as we watched him. A moment's silence, then the sinister left hand moves in, deep, foreboding, builds tension, gets louder and louder until the triumphant, powerful *fortissimo* climax, then back to the delicate theme. All this time, the audience dared not move or breathe, could not make a sound or turn away. We were transfixed.

. . .

In the dark of early morning in Paris, Frédéric's hand glides along my belly as I move in closer to him, but he isn't really awake. Soon his chest rises and falls in sleep, and I try to sleep, too. But I feel as agitated as I did before we came up here, though for different reasons now. Before, I was so anxious to be alone with him, so impatient for his touch, that I could barely think of anything else. Now I lie here and watch him, oblivious, exhausted, completely unaware of the turmoil I feel. He's also unaware of it when he's awake. I am simply the means to an end for him, the way he cannot be for me.

I vow not to let this happen again.

As I said, I don't think he understood what I felt for him, and I don't think I really understood what I felt for him either.

The last few months before he died, he would send me notes, sometimes odd and incoherent. At times I got the feeling he had been up too late, had a glass of wine too many, reflected too much perhaps on what might have been, and dashed off a note to me without thought. At first, I read too much into these notes, took him too seriously. I realized later that they meant nothing to him, were likely forgotten soon after they were written. Little did I know how soon I would regret not responding to them.

· · ·

In the spring of 1848 Liszt convinced Frédéric to go to London, where he believed he would have all the students he wanted, be able to give and attend concerts whenever he wanted, be embraced by the upper ranks of society. Instead, he spent a miserable seven months feeling alone, unable to speak the language, sick and broke. He returned to Paris as soon as his health would allow it, in November. A year later he would be dead.

Frédéric, always a great admirer of Mozart, had asked that the *Requiem* be sung at his funeral and wanted me to take one of the major parts. Women had never sung in La Madeleine before, and it took the church two weeks to decide to allow female singers to participate, provided they remained behind a black velvet curtain. I thought about it during those two weeks, changed my mind over and over. I had never given him an answer about it either way, always laughed it off, told him he'd get better. In the end I found I could not do it. I have regretted this decision from time to time. He would understand, I think.

· · ·

I realize I have missed my appointment. The sky grows dim, snow falls harder. I shake the accumulated flakes from my cape and consider going into Bisson Fils, trying to buy a copy of the photograph. Some part of me wants to possess this image of

Frédéric, keep it close. But another part thinks the moment cap-
tured in the picture is not what I want to remember of him: ill,
afraid, unhappy. I remember, then, about the two men Frédéric's
sister Ludwika told me about who came into his rooms to try to
take his photograph after he had died. Everyone present was so
grief-stricken and exhausted they didn't realize what the men
were trying to do until they moved his bed closer to the window
for better light. Ghouls.

The wind changes direction. Snow blows into my face now,
stings my eyes. Is leaving the photograph there like cutting my
heart out? Or like being buried alive? Perhaps having a copy
would be worse. I turn away, cross the street, decide I may return
for it another time. If I can stand it.

NURSE INGRID

Grey slush on the dirty brown carpet melts into puddles as I wait in the long checkout line with seniors and women with out of control kids and bargain hunters at the Bibles for Missions thrift store. I wonder why it's so busy, but then I remember it's the 30th, cheque day. I should have come yesterday.

"Morning," says Hedwig when it's my turn. Her name is printed in neat block letters with blue ballpoint on the name tag pinned to her high-necked off-white sweater, you could bounce a dime off her tightly permed blue-grey hair. I've been to the store so often lately I feel like I know her. She rings my purchases through and with each pair of panties—powder blue nylon grannies, black lace boy-cuts, hot pink bikinis, industrial-strength taupe control-panel jobs, no-nonsense white cotton briefs, red satin thongs—her lips purse a little harder, fine lines around them deepen. Finally, she can control her tongue no longer.

"These are all different sizes, you know."

I shrug. "I have a big family."

Her lips almost disappear. She rings the rest of my order through in silence, the cash register display reflecting in her glasses. She obviously doesn't believe me, but I don't give a damn what she thinks. It's none of her business. I leave the store with two plastic grocery bags full of panties, forty-four pairs at fifty cents a crack. Er, fifty cents each. Twenty-two bucks, and I've cleaned out their ladies' underwear bin for the second time in a month.

Next week, I'll hit Value Village for a change. Their prices are higher, but the kids who work there could care less what you buy, or why you buy it. Really, I just want to make a living. That's all any of us want, isn't it?

. . .

Snow whirls outside as Sunniva and Dana and I sit in front of my computer and nibble thick golden slices of Sunniva's *sockerkaka,* sponge cake. I have the computer in front of a window that overlooks the backyard so I can keep an eye on the boys when I'm using it. Dark-haired Dana looks a bit like a little girl, her feet dangling from the too-high-for-her barstool. She pushes her glasses further up her nose, reads aloud what she's typed so far. "Nurse Ingrid is lonely. She is Swedish, blonde, 5' 4", age twenty-six. She sounds a lot like you, Sunniva."

"Well. I'm a long way from twenty-six. And let's make her twenty-two."

"That seems kInd of young, don't you think?" I ask.

"Beth," says Sunniva. "What the hell difference does it make?"

"You're right. It doesn't matter." I sip my wine. "Thanks for bringing the cake, by the way. It's awesome."

"*Tack.* I'm glad you like it. How about this: She's lonely, twenty-two, and she loves to sell off her used panties in her own eBay store."

"Gently used?" I suggest.

"Lovingly used?" Dana muses.

"Let's just go with 'used' for now. We can always change it later," says Sunniva.

Dana raises her glass. "I'll drink to that."

"We should wrap this up for now," I say. "Almost time to pick up the kids."

．．．

Things have been better for me since Sunniva and Dana and I started hanging out together. But many days I still feel lost. Too often when Evan and Henry are at school, instead of doing some of the many millions of other things I should do, I find myself once again wandering Westbrook Mall. It's not that I want to shop for anything, particularly. I just don't want to be alone in the house, alone with my thoughts. I distract myself by fingering bright trinkets in the dollar store, by trying on clothes I have no intention of buying. Sometimes I don't recognize the woman looking back at me in the change rooms—she looks old and tired, with straggly red hair that hasn't been cut in months. In the noisy food fair, I sit with a cup of coffee and watch people come and go. Women with strollers and diaper bags and young children; sullen, dark-clad teenagers who should be at school; elderly couples who sit together, each lost to their own silences. Every once in a while I catch a glimpse of a tall man, and before I can stop myself I'll think it's Ian for a second, and in the next instant when I realize, of course, that it's not, I feel like my insides have been hollowed out.

Then it's time to go pick the boys up again. This new life as a widow is exhausting, bewildering, overwhelming. I wonder how I'll ever get used to it. The six weeks I've been off work are already almost up, and the college probably expects me to come back, or to tell them whether I am coming back or not. My boss, Charlotte, has been really good. But I don't feel ready to go back, I don't feel ready to do anything at all except sleep all hours of the day and night, heat up frozen food, and wander Westbrook Mall. I don't feel ready to make a decision about it. Everything seems to be out of my control. And it terrifies me.

But then there's Evan and Henry. They're my lifeline, all that keeps me from drowning. If I have no other reason to get it together, I have them. Only I have no idea how I can do it, how to even start.

. . .

We came up with the concept of Nurse Ingrid on one of our special Fridays. Dana's three-year-old, Peter, Sunniva's son John and my Evan and were all in the same preschool class, and Sunniva's Michael and my Henry were in kindergarten together. All boys, they got along so well. First, we started getting them together for playdates outside of school. Then the three of us started having coffee in the afternoons when they were all in school, which we found a lot more relaxing than playdates. Then the coffee became wine, on special Fridays, once or twice a month. After all, we could walk over to the school from my place. And those Fridays were indeed special. We needed them.

That day, the boys all wanted to go the playground after school, even though it was freezing out, and the three of us huddled near the school doors, tipsy and leaning against the brick wall, while they chased each other up and over and around the dizzyingly red, yellow and blue playground equipment.

Dana sighed. "Days like this I wish I could work from home. You see all these ads. You know, internet jobs. Work from home. Beth, didn't you make money selling stuff on eBay for a while?"

"Yeah, I did. It was kind of fun."

"You sold vintage clothes, right?"

"Yeah. And other stuff. Collectibles. I got a lot of it when I worked in a thrift store when I was in university. When the kids were little, I had to make some room, so I started selling off some of it."

"So why did you stop?"

"Partly because I ran out of things to sell, and I didn't have much time to pick up new stock in thrift stores. Partly because it's still a customer service job—you're always going to come across cranks and whiners who try to get something for nothing out of you. But mainly I quit because after a while the market got flooded with vintage stuff. I didn't make enough on each item to make it worthwhile."

"Maybe you just weren't selling the right clothes," Sunniva suggested. "A friend of mine told me her sister-in-law sells her used underwear on eBay. For a lot of money."

Dana's round grey eyes grew even rounder. "Really? How much?"

"Fifty, a hundred bucks a pair. She lists her auctions as 'Sexy college co-ed used panties', sells them to men all over the world."

I breathed out a low whistle.

"Come on, Beth. Are you shocked?"

"No. I'm figuring out the profit margin. Panties at the Bibles for Missions store are fifty cents a pair."

"Holy," said Sunniva in a little cloud of breath.

. . .

One special Friday we decide to get together in the evening. We order pizzas and Sunniva and Dana bring their kids over. After the kids eat, we plug them into *Finding Nemo* in the family room downstairs, their blond and red and brown heads lined up in a row in front of the TV. The three of us take care of a few Nurse Ingrid auctions that are about to end, then we relax with a drink.

"Cheers," I say. "Here's to Nurse Ingrid."

"She's bringing in a lot of money, isn't she?" asks Sunniva.

"She is. I never would have believed it. This is more money than I made working at the drugstore," Dana says.

"We'll see, but it looks like Sunniva and I may not have to go back to work, either," I say.

"Sunniva, why did you quit nursing?" Dana asks. "I mean, it's a good job."

Sunniva smiles. "It's hard work. And crazy hours."

"It must be stressful," I say.

"Stressful. Yes, well. That doesn't even start to describe some of it. You see a lot of things you hoped you'd never see, things you never imagined you'd see, when you work in emerg. And I did it for a lot of years.

"The thing, though, that pushed me over the edge…a man brought his little girl in late one night. Six years old, pretty little thing. She was bleeding very heavily. The father was white as a sheet, wouldn't tell us what happened. She just sat still, with her legs clamped together, wouldn't let us examine her, wouldn't answer any questions. We called the police, of course."

Sunniva's voice trails off. I want to say something, but I can't think what. Then she continues. "She died later that night and he was charged. I think in the end he was in jail for less than two years."

"Oh, Sunniva. That is so horrible."

"It is horrible. And I tried to forget about it. But I just couldn't. I felt sick every time I went in to work for a long time after that. It really frightened me, it still frightens me, to think that no matter how good our intentions are, no matter how hard we try to help people, there's so much that's out of our control."

Dana gets up. She is pale. "You know, I just realized the time. Mel is going to be back any minute. I should get home."

"Can't he get his own dinner?" asks Sunniva.

"I need to get home. I'm sorry," she mumbles, and goes downstairs to get Peter. He stomps up the stairs, whining that the movie isn't over.

"Peter. Control yourself," Dana says through her teeth. She's bent over, helping him jam his snow boots onto his feet, and I notice that one arm of her glasses is held on with duct tape. I am just about to ask her what happened to them when I think better of it.

I think Sunniva's story hit close to home for Dana, somehow. I'm sure Sunniva saw it, too, though we let it go, say nothing about it to each other.

. . .

Hedwig sees me come into the thrift store one morning and whips out from behind the counter with surprising agility, follows me down the housewares aisle, up the ladieswear aisle. She dips into the bin of men's socks, fires rolled up pairs at my head with the precision of a marksman. I try to scream but no sound comes out of my mouth, and I duck into the change room. As soon as I lock the door, she bangs her fists on it, yanks on the handle.

"You think you can hide in there, you panty-hoarding harlot. But you can't. You'll have to come out sooner or later."

Let go, let go of that door handle, I want to scream, and she rams into it with her shoulder.

I wake up covered in sweat. Clearly, there's a problem here.

. . .

On a Wednesday morning, I'm in the long line at the Starbucks at Westbrook Mall, telling myself this is it; this is the last time I will wander around here for no reason. I wish they had an express line for people who just want coffee. *Just give me a damn medium coffee,* I want to say. Instead I wait in line behind people ordering *grande, half-sweet sugar-free cinnamon dulce, non-fat, chai tea misto* or *tall Americano with a non-fat steamed topper*. Listening to them gives me a headache. And the couple in front of me, a beefy tattooed man in a hoodie and a slight dark-haired woman who wears a cropped t-shirt and tight pink pants, tight enough that she can't be wearing underwear, make out while they wait. They keep jostling me, no matter how far I move away. I'm about to say something when they get up to the counter and order *venti non-fat no whip classic hot chocolates, extra foam* or something.

Alas, when I take my damn medium coffee over to get a lid, the lovebirds are there. He has her up against the cream and lid station, her hands are down his pants. *Just get out of the fucking way*, I think. I try to reach around them for a lid, but I can't. My head throbs.

"Hey, take it somewhere else, would you?" I suggest.

The man spins around, roars, "Fuck *you*! Telling people what to do!"

"Charming," I mutter, and take my lid and leave. Should have sold her some panties while I was at it.

I meant to wander around the mall, but after that I take my damn medium coffee and go home. The experience leaves me a little shaken, feeling fragile. The guy was a total asshole. He could have slugged me, could have whipped out a gun, tough Starbucks gangsta that he obviously was. Then the whole thing could have spun out of control. I could have taken a bullet to the brain. And where would Evan and Henry be then? I would have to be extra careful from now on, that was all. As the only parent, caution was my only choice.

At home I sit down at the computer, decide that checking in on a few of our auctions will improve my mood. But there is an email from eBay. I read it a couple of times, then punch in Sunniva's number, stare at my computer screen in shock as she picks up.

"Hello?"

"Busted! Dammit, Sunniva, we're busted."

"Beth?"

"Yes! The panties. We're busted."

"What do you mean, busted?" she huffs. "There's no law against selling used clothes, is there?"

"No, there isn't. But eBay will no longer allow us to sell used panties. Health regulations or some bullshit. They sent out an e-mail. All our auctions are shut down."

"Fuck."

"I know."

Sometimes things happen and you realize maybe it's a blessing somehow. We all knew the Nurse Ingrid thing wouldn't last forever. But I think we wanted to be the ones to say it was time, we wanted to be in control of the ending. But there it was, pulled out from under us.

Now what the hell would I do with all those bags of panties? Re-donation seemed like the only answer.

. . .

After we receive the last payments from our happy customers before Nurse Ingrid suddenly disappears from eBay, we get together to split up the proceeds. It looks like it may be the last time the three of us will gather for a while; Dana's decided to leave Mel and she and Peter have moved in with her sister, on the other side of the city. She comes in my front door, stomps her snowy boots on the mat, has a huge red plastic Zeller's bag in her arms.

"What's all this? Stuff you're getting rid of for the move?"

"No." She nods at the bag. "Take a look."

I peer inside. The bag is full of panties. New cotton briefs, three to a package, sensible colours: white, ecru, black.

"Oh, my God."

"They had them on clearance. I just—I'm not really sure what got into me. Can you donate them to the thrift store for me? I won't have time to swing by there."

I try to imagine the look on Hedwig's face when I come in with this donation. "Yeah, no problem. How are you and Peter doing?"

"Good. You know. Pretty good. For now, I think living with Catherine's going to be the best thing for us. She works nights, so she can get him to and from school once I get a new job."

"Sounds like you're getting things under control."

"Yeah. It's going to be okay."

"Dana, we're not letting you go without having a drink and some *sockerkaka* with us," Sunniva says, pouring her a glass of wine. "Sit down. Besides, I have some news, too: I'm going back to work."

"Really? Where?" I ask.

"The General Hospital. It's a desk job, though, three days a week. Giving advice over the phone. I think I'll like it."

"Congratulations," Dana and I tell her. I'm happy for Sunniva, but surprised. I didn't see that coming at all.

. . .

After Sunniva and Dana leave, I rinse golden cake crumbs from our plates, rinse our wine glasses and put them in the dishwasher. There's still some time before I need to go pick up Evan and Henry, so I check my email. There's an email there from Charlotte at the college. I don't want to open it. I know what she wants. She wants me to tell her whether or not I'm coming back to work.

While I try to decide whether to open the message or not, I notice the Nurse Ingrid email file and decide it's time to delete it, time to let it go. And then that's it. The last trace of Nurse Ingrid is gone.

I get up, get my boots and coat, go out to pick up the boys. The sun has come out, the warmth feels good on my face. I decide I'll answer Charlotte's message after we get back. It's time now, I can do it. Besides, I tell myself, if I'm having a problem when I'm back at work, if things are getting out of control, I can always phone Sunniva for some advice. Somehow, knowing that makes me feel better.

GOOD FRIDAY, AT THE WESTWARD

Mike rubs the dark stubble on his chin like he's pondering a serious issue. "I think we got burned. These mushrooms aren't working," he says, and sinks deeper into the dull beige vinyl chair at our round orange table in the dim bar at the Westward Hotel. The rest of us are quiet for a moment before we start to laugh.

"Yeah, you're right. That must be why we've been here for half an hour and you've hardly touched your beer. And torn your coaster up into teeny tiny pieces," Tess says, rolls her china-blue eyes. Over and over, she pokes the maraschino cherry in the bottom of her orange and yellow tequila sunrise with her straw. It looks to me like she's stabbing at a bloody eyeball in her drink.

"What do you say, Cheryl?" she asks. "You're kind of quiet."

"Personally, I'm positive they're working." I say. They usually kick in pretty fast for me. Although I always have threatening waves of nausea and bouts of anxiety, cold, sweaty palms for half an hour or so before they start being fun. This particular night the anxiety seems worse, maybe because it's compounded by the Catholic-guilt voice in the back of my mind. "Mushrooms. A bar. On Good Friday." Am I having enough fun to risk going to hell for? So far, not even close.

Will, who until now has sat sullen and silent in the corner, speaks up. "I think we should blow this place. It sucks. We come here almost every weekend and we know the shows always start late. But none of the bands are even here yet and it's past ten. And this is the same stupid mixed tape they play before every show. I'm so sick of this tape."

He sounds cranky. I don't get it: he's the one who said we should come tonight because The Hai Karates, his new best friends from Vancouver, are supposed to be playing. Ever since he got back from Vancouver, he's seemed different to me. It's not just the new longer hair, the vague slogan t-shirts, the sparse beard he obsessively strokes tonight, like he's helping it grow or something. He has this attitude now, he's a snob all of a sudden. If he didn't still make my heart beat faster, I'd be mad at him. I guess I am mad; right now it's hard to tell. Oh Lord, why did he have to go away and turn into a hipster?

"Hey, man," says Mike. "You're the one who's all in with The Hai Karates. So where are they?"

"How am I supposed to know?"

"Okay. Take it easy. Anyone got any other ideas?"

"We could go to a movie," I suggest.

Will ignores me. He's good at that, been doing it a lot since he came back. "Steve's band is at the Bowness Hotel tonight. Why don't we get a cab and go over there?"

Before I know what's happening, we're crammed in a cab, got a ticket for our destination, and the anxiety creeps back up again. This isn't what we'd planned at all. We'd planned to take the mushrooms at Tess' and my place, walk a few blocks to the Westward and see some bands. Now we're on our way to the Bowness Hotel. It's far away. And I've never been there before. Isn't it scary, creepy, full of bikers and career drinkers? But the others seem calm, unworried. Of course, that's not unusual for Will. Nothing ever ruffles him. He's stubborn in his refusal to worry, or maybe that's how he wants to come off. Sometimes I think he does it just to aggravate me. But, no point in being upset now. The Bowness Hotel it is. Big, wet snowflakes swirl out of a dull purple sky and I take a deep breath as we pull into the parking lot.

. . .

Ye Olde Bowness Hotel: run-down, four bars, a big employer of bands. The biggest bar books country acts, one books hair bands, one's a sports bar, and the smallest is an old-timer hangout. Our friend Steve's country rock band is called The Hoedads. None of us are that partial to country music, but Steve's an old friend. They play non-threatening bar band stuff like The Eagles, Joe Walsh, Willie Nelson. We've seen them lots of times, and it turns out lots of people we know are here to see the band. I calm down a bit. With all the familiar faces this is a much more pleasant atmosphere than the Westward, even if it is far away.

During a set break I go to the washroom and see in the mirror that my pupils are huge. Stupid huge, people have got to be noticing that. When I come back to our table, Tess and Mike's pupils look just like mine. This strikes me as either a little sinister or very funny. As I try to decide whether or not to laugh, Tess says, "Someone at the next table said Bill Taylor and The Taylor Mades are playing one of the other bars here."

"Bill Taylor. Why does that name sound familiar?"

"Bill Taylor from The Roughriders."

"No way!"

"Yeah, c'mon. Let's finish our drinks and go check them out."

Will, who also has huge pupils says, "You girls go ahead. Mike and I are gonna stay here and shoot some pool."

My stomach knots up a little. What does that mean? That he really wants to play pool? That he thinks going to see The Taylor Mades is stupid? That he doesn't want to be around me?

Tess and I leave our coats, grab our purses, and go to find

The Taylor Mades. The snowflakes are smaller now, fall harder as we go from bar to bar. They aren't in the sports bar—obviously—or the hair band bar. We open the doors to the old-timer bar and step in out of the snow.

"Is this place even open?" I wonder. It's mostly dark, and empty except for two old men in plaid work shirts and truck logo baseball caps.

"I see people up on stage," Tess says.

Then the opening lick of "Evil Green Eyes" rings out and we know we're in the right place. "Evil Green Eyes" was one of The Roughriders' biggest hits. It seems kind of sad that they're here playing it all these years later for a couple of old guys in the corner who seem to ignore them. I feel a little uncomfortable, wonder if we should go back and see if The Hoedads are ready to start again. But Tess picks a table not too close to the front and we sit down.

"Evil Green Eyes" reminds me of the Flavoradio I had when I was a kid. The Christmas I was seven, my brother and I got Realistic Flavoradios, pocket transistor radios—blue for my brother, red for me. I had mine for years, went through a lot of 9V's obtained with my dad's Radio Shack Free Battery Club card. This was just after the CRTC brought in Can Con. So besides American and British music, we also heard "Sunny Days" by Lighthouse, "Evil Grows" by The Poppy Family, lots by The Guess Who and BTO. And of course, "Sweet Cherry Brandy" by The Roughriders.

Maybe it sounds weird, but I felt proud of The Roughriders when I was a kid. They weren't just a Canadian band, they were local. Western. Their first monster hit was "Sweet Cherry Brandy," and they had a string of others over the next few years. And, after several appearances on The Anne Murray Show, they even had a summer replacement show on CBC (which sadly wasn't picked up again).

And now here we are, catching them live (some of them, anyway) in the old-timer bar at Bowness Hotel. On Good Friday. On mushrooms. And I can't tell if this experience is really weird in and of itself or if I just think it is. It doesn't help that all four Taylor Mades wear buckskin shirts that give off a strange glow in the stage lights, complete with fringes and lace-up collars, like a bunch of aging Davy Crocketts. Bill Taylor looks older, no question. His black hair (two minutes for looking so good) is thin up front, long in the back, and he's stockier. His voice still sounds good, though. None of the other Taylor Mades seem to be former Roughriders. They all look younger than Bill. But the red-headed lead guitarist's fuzz-stung blues licks and easy harmonies with Bill's solid David Clayton-Thomas-like lead vocals are a pretty convincing recreation. I close my eyes for a second after the waitress takes our drink order and it's almost like listening to my Flavoradio again.

"Good evening. For those of you just joining us, we are Bill Taylor and The Taylor Mades." He purrs into the mike, looks straight at us.

"He's kidding, right?" Tess asks.

I try not to laugh. If he weren't looking right at us, I would. The Davy Crockett get-ups don't make it any easier. I feel like I have to nod and smile. I mean, obviously he's talking to us. The old guys in the corner drain their jug of draft in silence, stone-faced. Another song starts, one I don't recognize. Could be a lesser-known Roughriders song, a cover, a new original, hard to say.

When they finish Bill says, "Thank you. That's all from us for tonight, but we'll be back here again tomorrow, starting up at about eight o'clock. Hope you can make it out again."

Excellent, I think. Now we can finish our drinks and get back to The Hoedads. But then Bill and the guitarist come up to our table.

"You ladies mind if we join you?"

Oh, God. Go away, I think. *This can't be happening. This can't really be happening.* I glance at Tess. "Not at all," she says. Of course. I should have known. Tess has a thing for guys in bands, Mike or no Mike. It's like a game with her, or an addiction.

"I'm Bill, and this is Duane," he says as they sit down, Duane across from me and Bill across from Tess.

"I'm Tess, and this is Cheryl. We were at one of the other bars here and heard you were playing. So we had to come and check you out."

"Roughrider fans?" Duane asks.

"Oh, yeah," I say. "We've loved you guys since we were little kids."

Duane and Bill share a look, smile at each other. "Well, in that case, you'd better let us buy you a drink," Bill says as the waitress approaches. Holy shit. The Roughriders, buying us drinks. Never imagined that when I was a little kid. This can't be the right thing to do. On Good Friday, yet. The way they made me feel when I was a kid was a lot different, I have to say, than the way they're making me feel twenty years later. In the Bowness Hotel, on Good Friday, on mushrooms, they're making me feel nervous. Kind of icky. Like I want to go home.

This is all wrong. I just wanted to come and see what they looked like now, maybe hear "Sweet Cherry Brandy." I don't want to hang out with them. I don't want them to buy us drinks. I want to be back in the country bar with our friends, people we know, people our own age. People who'll make sure we get home. My stomach knots up. I must look uncomfortable because Tess elbows me and whispers, "Relax, Cheryl."

I take a deep breath as our drinks arrive. Ours look more like desserts than drinks. I usually stick to beer or wine. I don't know what these are, Paralyzers or Zombies, maybe. I have a couple of small sips. It's just too strange to drink this right now.

Tess chats away with Bill and Duane like they're old buddies. I have never understood how she does that, myself. Is it a blonde thing? But this isn't the first time I've been glad she's so talkative. It gives me a chance to sit back and observe. On the other hand, I also know that it's a mistake to let Tess do all the talking. When that happens, we always end up getting invited to party with the band, usually in their hotel room. You don't even want to know about the time Johnny Winter came to town and we somehow ended up hanging with his band. Let's just say the bass player thought Tess had the hots for him. I think she just wanted to steal his lizard-skin boots, the way she went on about them.

"A little quiet in here tonight," I say. As soon that's out, I realize how bad it sounds.

"Last time we play this dump," Duane says. "They didn't advertise this anywhere that I saw. The same thing happened last time."

Duane's shoulder-length hair falls in reddish waves around his face. Sometimes it seems to me that he's pretty handsome, but I'm not in any frame of mind to be able to tell. Maybe he isn't. One minute he looks like Jim Morrison, the next he looks like Van Morrison. Then sometimes he looks like Will. It's kind of disturbing.

Soon Bill and Duane and Tess order more drinks. I've finished about half of my drink, parfait, centerpiece, whatever the hell it is—it's not bad, actually—and now I have another. Bill shoots sly, brow-raised looks at Tess and me (practised so many times with so many women in so many bars), says, "So, ladies—Duane and I were wondering if you'd like to take the party up into our room."

As soon as he says that, the picture I've been trying to block out of my mind is suddenly all I can think of. I don't want to think about what Bill and Duane look like naked, but I can't help it. I don't want to think of nakedness right now, not any nakedness: theirs, mine or ours. I take a long sip of my drink—the new one, I somehow finished the first one.

The waitress comes by. Bill nods at me and says, "Another Paralyzer for the little lady."

Little lady? Jesus. We're back in the 70's for sure.

Tess grabs my arm. "Cheryl and I are just going to freshen up. We'll be right back."

. . .

"The Roughriders," she'd said in the washroom. "You're seriously going to give up a chance to party with the Roughriders?"

"It's just one real Roughrider. And he's old."

"Look. You'll regret chickening out for the rest of your life. Don't be such a coward."

Somehow, I have allowed Tess to talk me into it. So here we are up in Bill and Duane's grungy room. There are two double beds covered with shiny teal and dusty rose floral bedspreads, two teal upholstered chairs (I plan to stay on mine), pink lamps, a TV, a coffee table. It all smells suspiciously of air freshener. Bill puts a cassette in a portable tape player. Sounds like a pre-show mix: some blues, some old-time rock 'n' roll.

Since there's no fridge in the room, our resourceful musician friends have stocked the toilet tank with beer. Tess joins them in a frosty—er, drippy one. I'm still working on my Paralyzer, which I snuck upstairs under my coat. Now it's almost gone. I set my glass down on the table and try to figure out how I can get out of here and back to the country bar. Is it too late? Duane sits on the bed near my chair and sidles up as close to me as he can, plants his leg firmly onto mine.

"Well, darlin'," he says. "You're a shy one, aren't you?"

"I guess so." I'm trying to think of something else to say, something off-putting. He slides his hand over mine.

"Cold hands," he says. "Is it true what they say? You know—cold hands, warm heart?" I'm about to answer when the tape comes to the first driving chords of The Beatles' "Helter Skelter," and I realize who Duane actually reminds me of: Charles Manson.

Is it the incredibly corny line that finally moves me to action? I withdraw my hand, pull away from him, stand up. "Look," I say. "Before you get the wrong idea, I want to tell you right now that when I heard Bill Taylor and the Taylor Mades were here, all I wanted to do was come and check you out for a song or two. Maybe hear 'Sweet Cherry Brandy' and leave. I had no intention of letting you buy us drinks or partying with you."

As soon as I say that, everything is different. Not because of what I've said, though. It's different because all of a sudden, the whole room goes sideways. Across from us, the line where green carpet meets white wall wiggles a little, then dips and swoops. I break out in a cold sweat and know that I have maybe thirty seconds before I throw up. I make it to the bathroom, pull the door shut behind me before I lose it all in the toilet: the remains of the pizza we had for dinner, the mushrooms, the beer and the Paralyzers. I managed it pretty neatly though, nothing on my clothes. A little wiping around the toilet and it's cleaned up. I feel better for a minute or so, take a deep breath.

. . .

I open my eyes, see snow swirl from pinkish clouds out a cab window. It's quiet and warm, and I lean up against someone's arm. For a second I think it might be Duane, but then I look up and see it's Will.

"Where are we going?" I ask.

"Home. How are you doing?"

"Better than before. I'm kinda tired now."

"No kidding. What the hell happened there?"

"I don't know. We went to see The Roughriders and the next thing we know they're buying us drinks. Paralyzers. I guess I had too many."

"So I gathered."

"I didn't even feel good to start with. And I didn't want to party with them."

"Uh-huh. I forgot to ask Tess whether any of them had lizard-skin boots."

We pull up in front of the apartment building. "You want me to come in?" Will asks.

We climb the stairs, I drink water, use the bathroom and get into bed with Will. He shuts off the lights and I see his silhouette against the soft glow of the yellowed blind behind him.

"Jesus Christ, Cheryl. Look after yourself," he says, and kisses me. I don't recall whether I brushed my teeth or not just now, hope I don't taste like puke.

For a little while I think I won't be able to sleep. The whole crazy night or week or whatever plays over and over in my head. Then I drop off and start to dream right away. In the dream I sleep almost two days straight. But on the third day, I rise again.

THE UNCHANGING SEA

March 1910

A thin ham sandwich wrapped in wax paper, a piece of cheese, an orange and a small bottle of milk made up the meagre boxed lunch the Biograph Company provided for us actors.

"Mr. Griffith and Billy Bitzer always eat at a pub in town," my sister Joan grumbled as the ocean breeze tumbled her blonde ringlets into her eyes. "And we're supposed to last all day on this."

As I finished my orange, I noticed another actor leaning up against the side of a truck, taking big bites out of his sandwich. That one sandwich couldn't have been much of a meal for a big man like him. Well, not so much big; tall, and very lean. Over his high, sharp cheekbones his eyes were set deep. I couldn't see what colour they were, but his skin was fair, and his wavy, dark hair straggled in the wind. He stroked his beard and talked with another man as he ate. I noticed his wide, open smile. Juice dripped into his beard when he bit his orange.

Joan touched my arm. "Flora, let's get in line for the toilet."

"You go. I'm all right."

"We won't get a chance again for hours. C'mon."

"In a minute. I want to finish my milk."

"Suit yourself."

When we arrived at the beach shortly past five that morning, a dim glow had just begun in the east. It was too dark to tell the difference between the sea and the sky. We all waited for Mr. Bitzer to set up his camera. He and D.W. Griffith had come to the fishing village of Santa Monica to shoot a moving picture called *The Unchanging Sea,* based on the poem "The Three Fishers" by Charles Kingsley. I thought about the irresistible force of the tides going in and out forever, how the sea is unchanging.

Joan said Biograph would pay us ten dollars each for just two days' work and give us lunch, too. I didn't really believe her, but in the past year she'd worked for Kalem, Selig and Essanay, other moving picture companies that had come to California from New York to take advantage of the sunlight and the mild weather. I'd been on stage a couple of times before but never made that kind of money, and this sounded a lot easier to me. Moving pictures had no lines to memorize, and we were just extras. Even though Joan liked working in pictures, I wasn't sure what to think of them. Everyone said it would ruin your chances for a real career in the theatre. It did all sound a little too good to be true, the money, the easy work. But I thought I'd try it once, at least.

It turned out the work wasn't as easy as Joan made it sound. We stood on the windy shore from sunrise until sunset both days; mid-March was not yet all that warm. This man Griffith shot the same scene over and over, and after a while I don't think any of us had a clue what he wanted.

. . .

Back at the beach at sunrise the next morning, I tied my loose boot laces as we waited for Mr. Bitzer to set up the camera again. I heard a man's voice behind me, low and gentle.

"Arise, fair sun, and kill the envious moon, who is already sick and pale with grief, that thou, her maid, art far more fair than she."

I straightened up. The tall man from the day before smiled at me, touched his hat brim.

"*Romeo and Juliet,*" I said.

"The sunrise put it in my mind. I toured in a production last fall."

"Really? I heard Mr. Griffith likes to hire stage actors."

"Yes. And my wife likes the money I make working for Biograph. Everyone's happy this way."

"I see you've met Keefe," said Joan. Her eyes darted from me to the man, then back again.

"Well, we hadn't really introduced ourselves yet," I said.

"Allow me. Mr. Keefe Hanson, this is my sister, Mrs. Flora Bailey."

"Pleased to meet you, Mr. Hanson."

"Likewise, Mrs. Bailey," he said, and took my hand in a firm grip. I could see now that his eyes were blue, the blue of the sky on a warm day, as they flickered up and down my body. "I look forward to working with you."

I didn't know where to look. "Yes. I do, too."

. . .

We had just finished the fifth take of a scene where a group of us were being filmed from the back as we gazed out at the ocean. Keefe joined me on a bench in the shade. Though he touched my arm lightly, it jolted through me like electricity. "Mrs. Bailey, your sister tells me that you love poetry."

"I do. Very much, Mr. Hanson." He smelled faintly of tobacco and bay rum and sweat.

"Keefe. So, then who is your favourite poet?"

"That's a hard question. I love so many poets. Walt Whitman, Longfellow, Matthew Arnold. But I think my absolute favourite is Browning."

"Perfect. I have a Browning poem for you."

And he recited "Porphyria's Lover" with perfect expression and pacing, his eyes on me the whole time. I could not take my eyes off him, and only noticed near the end that a small crowd had gathered to listen.

He finished, "And thus we sit together now, and all night long we have not stirred, And yet God has not said a word!"

After a little applause we went back to work. But "Porphyria's Lover" stayed in my head, in Keefe's low, smooth amber voice, for days afterward.

. . .

The next day we thought the shoot would never end, but by evening we finished *The Unchanging Sea*. Keefe and I had got to talking near the end. Most people scattered after Linda Arvidson gave us our pay. Not only was Linda the lead actress in the film, playing the woman who watches and waits for her lost husband year after year, I later found out she was also Mr. Griffith's wife. The two had kept their marriage a secret, ostensibly so as not to harm their theatrical careers. But when they divorced a few years later, I wondered if there were other reasons one or both of them wanted to keep the marriage a secret. I know I happened to be near her when someone made a remark about the uplifting moral themes Mr. Griffith liked in his pictures. Linda snorted and said almost under her breath, "Funny, isn't it?"

Somehow Keefe and I had managed to have a running conversation going about poetry all day, whenever we could fit it in. Imagine, having a conversation with someone about poetry. It had been a very long time since I'd had a conversation of any kind with a man, but one about poetry, of all things. And a conversation about poetry with a handsome, articulate man. This had never happened to me before.

"I suppose I ought to find my sister and go now. But I've enjoyed talking to you," I said.

"And I've enjoyed talking to you. In fact, this whole day reminds me of a poem I once wrote," he said.

"You write poetry? Have you ever had any of it published anywhere?"

"Well, no. I've sent a few poems out, but they always come back. My wife says I'm wasting my time."

"I'd love to read some of them sometime. I studied poetry in college."

"Do you? That's very interesting."

Joan came by, looked at Keefe long and hard for a second and then at me. "Flora. C'mon, the bus back to town is leaving in a few minutes."

"Yes. Yes, I should go." I didn't want to. Something pulled me toward him. My eyes followed the full curve of his lips.

"Are either of you working on the next film?" he asked as we walked over to the bus.

"Linda said she'd forgotten to ask you, Flora, but if you want to work again tomorrow, they could use us both," Joan said.

"Oh. Well, yes, I think I'd like to," I said.

"Good," said Keefe. "Then this isn't goodbye. It's just until tomorrow. Goodnight, ladies."

I watched as he walked away and out of view.

"Flora? Listen, I know Keefe is handsome. And charming. But watch out for him," Joan began.

"Joan. I'm your older sister. Don't worry about me."

"All right."

. . .

"Bailey, what's this about your wife acting in the flickers?" Mr. Swanson, the bank manager, Charles's boss, asked between courses at a dinner party at his house one night. Though I sat right beside the man, he couldn't have asked me.

"Keeps the little wife busy," Charles laughed. "Flora's always been one of these arty types. She loves poetry, music, theatre, all that kind of thing."

Mr. Swanson coughed, poured himself more wine. "Wise to let them have a hobby. Keeps them occupied. Isn't that right, Marcelle?"

His wife gave a tight and forced smile, eyes on her plate. "Of course, dear."

We don't go to many parties. Charles likes nothing better than to fall asleep after dinner with his paper and his brandy. I suppose I should be grateful that he doesn't object to my acting. Some would say he indulges me, as though I were a spoiled child or a pet. If only he paid me as much attention as he would a child or a pet. It's more that he doesn't care what I do, as long as it has no effect on him. Sometimes I wonder why we ever married. I'm certain now that he would have preferred a solitary life. But how would that have looked? How would his mother, the dear, have stood it? And most importantly, who would cook and clean for him?

Many people suffer a great deal more than I do; I know that. My life isn't so bad, not really. But then why do I feel this enormous longing for Keefe, a longing like I've never felt before, like I never would have believed it possible to feel? Why do I feel so sad? I go over it and over it in my mind and I can't understand it, start to think that I'll never understand anything anymore. Charles would say I'm being melodramatic again. Then he'd yawn and go back to his newspaper.

I suppose it happened because of the sorry state of things between Charles and me, at least partly. Of course, we were in love when we married, hard as that seems to remember now. But as the years went by and it became clear we would remain childless, it seemed Charles no longer found intimacy necessary. Several years ago, he moved into his own bedroom, said he had trouble sleeping and didn't want to keep me up. That upset me at first, although I've grown used to it, as I've grown used to seeing him for only an hour or so in the evening over dinner. Then, most evenings, he reads the newspaper and falls asleep in his armchair, while I read poetry. In silence, except for the ticking of the hall clock that marks the passing of our lives minute by minute. Day after day, week after week, year after year.

Little by little things changed, we talked less, shared less. It happened so slowly that I barely noticed. Until I met Keefe. Somehow, until then, I didn't even understand how lonely I'd become. But what could I do? I could never even mention a divorce, Charles being brought up a Catholic. Though God knows we rarely go into a church from one year's end to the next, except to go to a wedding or a funeral.

It's odd, but in my heart, I never felt that loving Keefe was wrong. If it was wrong, why did I feel with everything in me that I needed him? If what I felt was wrong, why did God make me this way? I thought many times of Walt Whitman: "Two hawks in the air, two fishes swimming in the sea not more lawless than we." Keefe seemed to me like an irresistible force of nature, something I had no power over, no choice about.

. . .

The next week we shot a Western. Pictures in those days were one reel long, and sometimes Biograph made two or three one-reelers a week, same crew, same actors. Mr. Griffith's favourite ingénue at the time was Mary Pickford. If the almost constant attention he paid her bothered Linda Arvidson, she never let on, at least not to us. Miss Pickford was cast as an Indian maiden in this picture, because of her high cheekbones, Joan said.

I was glad of the fuss he made over her, because it allowed us extras more time away from the camera. And that day I felt tired. I hadn't been sleeping well, and the previous night had been particularly bad. Several times in the middle of the night

I woke with thoughts of Keefe, heard his voice, saw the glow of the rising sun on his hair. Now we leaned against a boulder together and talked while Mr. Griffith tried different camera angles, adjusted Miss Pickford's wig and costume over and over. We spoke of inanities at first, but suddenly Keefe grew serious.

"Flora, listen to me." His eyes reflected the blue of the sky as he looked away from me toward the hills, and almost whispered, "My wife—cannot."

Questions rushed through my mind. *Cannot what? Are you saying what I think you're saying? Why are you telling me this?* As I tried to think how to respond, I became aware of a hush around us.

Mr. Griffith glared at us. "If Mr. Hanson and Mrs. Bailey are finished chatting, perhaps we can all get back to work. Would that be all right with you two?"

Back in school for a moment, I hung my head, moved away from Keefe. He coughed, said, "Yes. Er, sorry, sir."

. . .

Shooting on the Western would wrap up that Friday, a warm day. Since Keefe and I weren't in some shots, we found a shady spot. He said a director at Kalem was planning a film about the life of Jesus Christ and wanted to cast Keefe as Judas Iscariot.

"Didn't Judas have red hair?" I asked.

I noticed his straight, slightly rounded teeth when he laughed. "Yes. But it's hard for the audience to tell what colour your hair is. They could give me a wig, you know."

"I suppose so." Of course they could. It just seemed like such an odd part for Keefe, being so sweet and dear.

He cleared his throat, moved in a little closer to me, spoke softly. "It's hard to talk at work here. We're always being interrupted."

"Yes. Yes, it is hard to talk."

"We should meet somewhere where we can talk," he said.

I swallowed, looked down at my hands and then back at him. "I would like that."

He came closer and kissed me. He tasted a little of tobacco. Then Mr. Griffith's voice broke in on us, unusually shrill.

"Extras! We need you all now!"

"Are you quite ready, Mrs. Bailey?" he asked as we returned.

"Yes, sir."

Keefe coughed, said nothing. His eyes looked different. Now they were a cold blue.

We went back to work.

. . .

All weekend my mind raced. Where could we meet, when? How would it ever work? I tried to remain hopeful. Love would find a way.

Keefe did not come to work Monday morning. My heart sank and I thought again of Walt Whitman: "From plenty of persons near and yet the right person not near." Perhaps he'd just slept in—it was very early, still dim, though the eastern sky glowed dull orange. I heard the faint crowing of a rooster somewhere. Then Linda touched my arm.

"Flora. Mr. Griffith asked me to speak to you."

I felt it must be something about Keefe. I pictured him lying ill in bed and my insides knotted up.

She let out a long breath. "Mr. Hanson spoke to Mr. Griffith on Friday. Keefe—uh, Mr. Hanson—said you've been throwing yourself at him. He says it's making him uncomfortable."

Uncomfortable. I felt dizzy and sick. My face grew hot. I could not speak.

Linda looked me in the eye. She had the roundest blue eyes I'd ever seen. "Mr. Griffith saw you kiss him. You do know that he will not tolerate moral laxity in his players."

At that she dropped her gaze. "He's asked me to thank you for the work you've done for Biograph. We'll pay you for today, but under the circumstances we can't use your services anymore." She put her hand over mine. "I'm sorry to have to be the one to tell you. It's a shame Keefe isn't man enough to talk to you himself. I'm so sorry, Flora."

Something rushed out of me then. I was still dumbstruck, likely a blessing. On the bus home as I clutched my five dollars, her words rang in my ears.

I didn't cry until much later. Over the next weeks, shame, hurt, anger coursed through me. I thought of telling my side of the story, of retaliation, of revenge. But doing these things would only diminish whatever was left of my dignity.

For a long time, something drew me back to the beach. Sometimes I think I dreamed it all, it seems so strange now. I've realized the sea is not unchanging. The sea is actually unpredictable. The shells and creatures that wash up on the shore change constantly. The tide is ever-changing. The water can be still as glass one moment, raging the next. The colour shifts always: deep grey, slate green, dark blue. Cold sea wind, warm blue sky. Cold blue eyes.

THE HARDEST PART

On an October afternoon, air clear as a bell, yellow leaves twirling down, I sipped coffee on my deck, soaked in the sun's weak autumn rays.

I got the news about you via Facebook.

Your sister Alma and I hadn't seen each other in almost forty years, though we 'liked' and 'shared' each other's posts. "We are heartbroken to say," she wrote, "that our dear brother Rob passed on Tuesday."

Jesus. What? I took a breath before I read more, pulse pounding in my ears.

"A celebration of Rob's life will be held at St. Gertrude's Church on Oct. 19th at 7 PM."

I stood up, paced mindlessly for a minute. Had a glass of water. Cursed. Read it again a few times in case I'd missed something, like maybe it was someone else, some other Alma I knew in high school who also had a brother named Rob.

You weren't the first of our little circle to 'pass', as Alma put it. Margo swallowed pills while we were still in high school; Ben veered onto the wrong side of a country road late at night; Duane did a Jimi Hendrix, passed out at a party. As we got older the toll became more predictable, the kinds of fate associated with aging: cancers, heart attacks, strokes.

When our old friend Matt passed a couple of years ago, it hit me hard. You and I talked about it briefly, again on Facebook.

"Lung cancer. Couldn't have seen that coming," you said.

"You're evil, Rob."

"It was inevitable the way he smoked, that's all. No surprise. Nothing we can do about it now."

I'd forgotten how cold you could be. Later, when my anger softened, I thought perhaps you were in shock, or masking your feelings behind unkindness. As was your wont. You and Matt were close at one time, so close that people talked. Not that you and I had been close recently—I wonder how close you ever let anyone get—but it's been clear to me for a long time that you dealt with intimacy by minimizing it, pretending it didn't happen.

I wish I'd understood that when I was eighteen.

. . .

Winter night. Kitchen party in an ancient, rundown rental house downtown. Some came from clubs after seeing bands, some came after a movie at the Plaza. They kept coming and coming. The kitchen got crowded, the music got louder: *Eat to the Beat*, a new album just out. We stepped, you and I, into the unlit back porch, sat on a stack of boxes, far from the madding crowd. The music muffled, Deborah Harry's ice-queen vocals on "Sound A Sleep" a background lullaby for an all-nighter. Frost-whorled windowpanes silhouetted us; our words formed clouds in the purple hush.

"It's cold," you whispered. "Come closer."

. . .

Jobs, family, moves. I eventually had the jobs and the family, you seemed to move a lot. You left town and came back how many times? The first time felt like it would kill me. Now those days seem far off and small. For many years we lost touch, but as time goes by there seems to be a pull from the past. Maybe for no other reason than to prove to yourself it really happened, for better or worse. Or perhaps it's an attempt to remember being young? Whatever the reason, our paths crossed a few times in the last ten years, purposefully, accidentally, sometimes both. Then social media came along and made it far too easy, far too instant, to share bits of our lives, to react blindly to news, even personal news. To stay connected, sometimes daily, with people that in previous eras you would have long ago forgotten.

Though I don't expect that would have happened with us.

. . .

To many people, music is background noise. A few don't notice music at all. To me, that would be like being dead. I am always aware of any music I hear, and how it makes me feel. One day after work at a job I had after high school, my brother picked me up. It was hard, hot, dusty work, packing boxes, stacking pallets in a windowless warehouse, and the drive home was long. The opening notes of a song I hadn't heard before riveted my attention to the radio, and I turned it up.

The sustained bass notes, the tambourine, the tinny Rickenbacker guitar all suggested the Byrds, 60's folk-rock, sounding like none of the overproduced, synthesized AM radio pap that was pop music in the early 80's. If I loved the sound of the song, I loved the lyrics even more. I felt like they were directed at me, like my wait was over and finally I was getting something going with you. That evening you and I would go out again, to another movie and then back to your place.

"That's a new song called 'The Waiting' from Tom Petty and the Heartbreakers," the DJ said.

That day I didn't know that in only a few short weeks, you would leave town for the first time, that what we had going would be finished almost before it had begun. My heart was soaring so high right then I don't think I would have believed it.

. . .

I hadn't been inside a church in many years, not since my father's funeral. My mother didn't want a funeral. She asked us to scatter her ashes in the sea. St. Gertrude's, as it turned out, wasn't St. Gertrude's anymore but was now called the Gaia Community Gathering Centre. The celebrant, who introduced himself as Gareth, was much younger than us, wore a plaid flannel shirt and wire-rimmed glasses. His eulogy was about you, I suppose, but little of what he said seemed specific to you; he mostly seemed to be reciting vaguely comforting platitudes that sounded as though they'd been lifted from self-help books and inspirational social media memes. "Let yourself feel all the emotions around this grievous loss," he counselled, "and then release them. It's what Rob would have wanted."

Seriously? It's what you would have wanted? I never recalled you giving much of a damn about other people's emotions. Clearly, someone wanted a service—your sister Alma, perhaps—and they got one. But I couldn't imagine you wanting any of this yoga-class-cum-memorial-service.

As Gareth continued, my mind wandered. My eyes fixed on the urn beside the altar. The last of you. People all around me crying, and I felt like I ought to, too, but the tears didn't come. Proof, I thought, that I was, at last, well and truly over you.

A small part of me welcomed the chance to reconnect in person with some of our friends from the old days. But the rest of me was dying to get away from all these people I didn't know. Even those I had known—it was so long ago we might as well have been strangers. Then there was your family who, besides Alma, I'd never met, and some of the many friends you'd gathered before and after the brief parts of our lives that we shared.

Before the crowd began streaming out, I decided I couldn't join them at the wake, although Alma had invited me. Alma's long hair was still dyed jet-black like she'd had it in high school.

Though her dingy black thrift store Jackie O suit—edgy, ironic when she was eighteen—now seemed odd as she approached sixty. None of us ever imagined getting this old, and we never imagined how quickly it would happen. It hit me that I had nothing to say to her or anyone else here; I needed to be alone with my sadness. I slunk out before the service ended. Gareth's voice faded as the double doors into the narthex closed behind me and disappeared altogether as I descended the steps and slipped into the now-dark parking lot. I hadn't cried yet, not through the whole service. I didn't want to cry, not there, not then.

I pulled out of the parking lot and navigated through the unfamiliar suburban area. Once I got back to a main drag, I switched the radio on to quell the flood of thoughts in my head. The opening of the song was unmistakable: the sustained bass notes, the tambourine, the tinny Rickenbacker. It was, of course, "The Waiting" by Tom Petty, whom we lost a week earlier. It wasn't bad enough that you were gone. Now Tom Petty, too? Fuck.

I found an empty parking lot in front of a boarded-up music shop, stopped the car and cried. You were gone, Tom Petty was gone, and yes, that all made me sad. But I was really crying about the innocent hope that song had brought up in my heart, the hope that had died so soon after. I was mourning what could have been.

Then another song came on, something so bland I've already forgotten it. Probably Phil Collins. I switched off the radio, dried my eyes, blew my nose and drove home into that good night.

ASK YOUR MOM

My best friend Christie and I were coming back from the store one Saturday afternoon—the Chinaman's, my mom called it, as in, 'Rachel, go to the Chinaman's and get me some cigarettes.' It was down our street and around the corner, about halfway down the block. Today I wasn't getting any cigarettes, though. Christie and I both bought watermelon gum. They came three to a bag and were green striped on the outside and pink on the inside. They didn't really taste like watermelon, but they were sweet, and kind of sour, too.

Lots of people thought we were sisters. Her hair was brown and mine was blonde, and she was a year older than me. I was afraid of the big, black dog in the front yard of the house beside the store. Christie wasn't. She said they used to have a dog, Tinkerbell, who got run over. This day it was too hot for the dog to run up to the fence like it usually did. It sat on the verandah and barked instead.

The house was two storeys, white, and the upstairs windows had brown shutters with silhouettes of sailboats cut into them. One of the shutters hung by one hinge, looked like it would fall off.

Christie nodded at the house as we walked by. "A girl in my class lives in that house. Her name is April Muller." Christie had just finished grade one and I would start in the fall.

She continued. "She used to have a little brother. Stephen."

"What happened to him?"

"He died."

"How?"

"He bit his own wiener."

I was confused. "He died from biting his own wiener?"

"He bit it and he swallowed the pee. It poisoned him. They took him to the hospital, but it was too late."

I didn't say anything else. It sounded kind of crazy, but it seemed like the world was full of crazy things. And I had a little brother. One thing I definitely knew about boys—they were weird.

When I went back into our house around supper time, I knew my mom and dad had been arguing. They had arguments a lot, sometimes little ones that they thought I didn't notice. They'd talk through clenched teeth, or sometimes didn't talk to each other at all. Even though they were trying to pretend they weren't mad when they did that, I knew just because they weren't yelling at each other didn't mean they weren't having an argument. This one might have been a big one, one of the ones that just seemed to start like something exploding. They didn't even try to pretend those ones weren't happening. They'd launch into yelling, screaming, throwing stuff, crying and it was like Wayne and I weren't even there. We'd go outside if it was nice out, or daytime. But sometimes we just had to stay in our bedroom. There wasn't anywhere else to go. We could hear every word they said through the thin walls.

This one looked like it was over, mostly. *Wide World of Sports* was on, but my dad wasn't really watching it. The TV flickered in his glasses. The muscles in his cheek rippled as he blew smoke out his nose and looked out the window. Mom was making supper. She slammed the cupboard doors shut, banged the pots onto the counter. I thought she'd break the plates the way she threw them on to the table.

"Rachel!"

Before I answered, I tried to think—what had I done? Was it something about me they were fighting about? "Yes, Mom?"

"Go find your brother."

Wayne wasn't four yet, but sometimes it would take me a long time to find him. Sometimes that was good. Sometimes I thought Wayne was a lot smarter than me.

Wayne and Dennis from down the street were crouched at the end of the alley, their blond pig shaved heads almost touching.

"Wayne, it's time for supper."

"Wait a minute. Look at this."

They were poking with sticks at something on the sidewalk. "What is it?"

"We got it out of a robin's nest," Dennis said.

A baby bird spilled out of a blue shell. It had huge, closed eyes that would never open, transparent skin, no feathers.

"You killed it."

"We thought it was ready to hatch," said Wayne.

I had to stop looking at the dead baby. It hurt to look at it. "C'mon, Wayne. We have to go."

When we got home, Mom gave Wayne and me our suppers, said nothing.

"Where's Dad?" Wayne asked. I'd been thinking about the baby bird, forgot about Mom and Dad.

"He went out for a beer with Gil. Eat your supper."

Wayne opened his mouth like he was going say something else, but I kicked him under the table. I could see that Mom was not in the mood for more questions.

. . .

The next day was Sunday, another hot day, and we had to go to church, like we always did on Sunday. I wished there was a Baby Jesus to look at in this church, because I liked babies. But there was only the old, scary Jesus on the cross, and the other sad one with his heart on fire. The crinoline Mom made me wear under my dress was hot and itchy, and I knew if I tried to scratch in church I'd get in trouble. Once communion was over, every time we got up from sitting or kneeling, I'd think it must be the end of the mass, but it seemed to keep going on and on. Finally, though, the priest said, "In the name of the Father, and of the Son, and of the Holy Ghost," and we all answered, "Amen."

Lately, when we crossed ourselves in church, I wondered what would happen when I developed. Was there a special way ladies did it so that you didn't accidentally touch one of them? I watched my mom and the other women as they crossed themselves, but none of them ever seemed to accidentally touch one. I was sure I would, and it would be awful. Maybe you had to practise in front of a mirror for a while to get the hang of it.

After lunch I called on Christie. She said it was too hot to go out and we should play in the basement. Christie had a lot of Barbies, but her little sister Tillie had cut the hair off almost all of them. So her mom knitted hats for them. We played Barbies behind the big stack of boxes of Pablum in the middle of the rec room floor. Rows and rows of pink-faced babies with spoons in their mouths stared at me and Christie and the toque-wearing Barbies.

"Why do you have all this Pablum? Isn't Tillie too old to eat it?"

"It's not for Tillie. My dad's a salesman and those are samples he has to take with him when he goes out of town." Christie's dad was Gil, the guy my dad went out for beer with sometimes.

I didn't say anything else, but it made me a little mad to know that the Kendalls had all this baby food in their basement, and my mom was about to have a baby, and they didn't give us any. Come to think of it, Mrs. Jeworski from next door had a new baby, and so did Kenny's mom. All these babies around, and all this Pablum in the Kendalls' basement. It didn't seem right to me.

"Christie," Mrs. Kendall called down the stairs. "Tillie's going down for a nap right now, and I need it to be quiet in here, so you girls go play outside."

There was a big tree in Christie's front yard. We sat in the shade and smashed our leftover watermelon gums with big rocks. The ones we'd chewed tasted good at first, but once you chewed all the sugar out of the gum it was stiff and kind of bitter. Ants came, red and black, and crawled all over the smashed gum. We poked them off with sticks and they kept coming back.

Two older boys from down the street came by on bikes and stopped in front of us. One had red hair and freckles and the other had black hair and black-rimmed glasses. Christie knew them from school, but I didn't. I felt kind of shy of them. They talked to Christie, who laughed at the jokes they told, but I kept quiet. After a while the one with glasses asked me what my name was. Before I could answer, Christie said, "Her name is Rachel. She's not in school yet."

"Hey, Rachel. Do you know what a cunt is?"

I'd never heard the word before. I looked at Christie, but she just shrugged. "No," I answered.

The red-haired one spoke up. "Why don't you go ask your mom?"

"Why don't you ask *your* mom, Christie?" After all, we were in her yard.

"Tillie's sleeping and my mom doesn't want any noise."

"Oh, yeah. Okay," I said, getting up to cross the street. "I'll be right back."

It wasn't much cooler inside our house than it was outside. Mom was watching TV on the couch.

"Mom," I said. "What's a cunt?"

Her face went all white, and she stood up and stared at me. She looked really mad and for a minute I thought I was about to get it.

"Where did you hear that word?"

"Two big boys came up to Christie and me and asked us if we knew what it meant."

"Just now?"

I nodded.

She was out the front door before I even knew what happened. I couldn't hear exactly what she said, but she was yelling at the boys. I was glad she wasn't yelling at me. I looked out the screen door and saw the boys ride away on their bikes, and my mom came back into the house red-faced to the roots of her dark brown hair.

"Don't you ever say that word again."

I still didn't know what it meant, but I could tell it was something bad.

. . .

My mom and dad hadn't been talking to each other since he went out for a beer with Christie's dad. At least that was quieter than when they were yelling, but it still wasn't any fun. If they wanted to talk now, they'd talk to me and I was supposed to talk for them.

"Christie, ask your dad to pass the sugar, please."

"Tell your mom I'm going out tonight so don't wait up for me."

Part of me wanted to ask them why they did this, why they made me part of their fight when they knew I didn't want to be. But I knew I couldn't. I was just supposed to do what they told me to, no questions. I was supposed to be a good girl. But when they acted like that I wanted to take off and stay away all day the way Wayne did.

. . .

A few days later we were playing in Christie's basement again to be out of the afternoon heat.

"Come and see this calendar my Dad's got," Christie said.

We went into a part of the Kendall's basement I hadn't seen before. There was a bench with tools hanging on the wall behind it. And a calendar with a picture of a lady sitting on a leopard-skin couch. She had long red hair and orange lipstick and wore a black nightie and held a drink in a fancy glass. Then Christie lifted up something and suddenly the lady had no clothes on. The black nightie was just printed on a piece of clear plastic. Christie flipped the plastic back and forth and the lady's nightie appeared and disappeared. I was speechless.

"My dad thinks I don't know," Christie said, "but he has a whole box of magazines with pictures of naked ladies like this in the garage."

I wondered if our dads looked at pictures like these when they went for beers. Probably. That must have been why they couldn't just drink beer at home. That's what Mom always asked him, why couldn't he just have a beer at home? Now I knew why. No wonder Mom was mad at him.

. . .

A few days later Christie and I played hopscotch on the sidewalk in front of her house when the same two big boys came up to us on their bikes again.

"Hey, Rachel," the one with glasses said. "Did your mom tell you what a cunt is?"

"No."

He looked across the street at my house to see if my mom was around. They began to pedal away, but he turned around just before they ducked into the alley and said, "It's a girl's dink."

A girl's dink? I was so confused. So was Christie. As far as we both knew, girls didn't have dinks.

A little while later Christie had to go in, so I went home. And even though I wanted to ask my mom, or someone, about the whole girl's dink issue, I knew I didn't dare.

When I came into the living room, Mom and Dad were lying on the couch and kissing. I don't think they even noticed me. I knew this was another one of those times not to talk to them, same as when they were fighting. I went through the kitchen and out the back door and sat on our swing set.

After a while I heard some stirring in the kitchen. Mom must have been starting to make supper. "Christie," she called out the screen door. She probably wanted me to go to the cellar to get some potatoes or set the table, or maybe go to the store to get something.

I kicked at the dirt under the swings for a minute as Wayne and Dennis ran laughing past our back fence. Mom called me again. But before she saw me, I slipped through the back gate and down the alley. My heart pounded as I ran free after my brother, and I laughed, too.

AWKWARD POSITIONS

My nephew Ben squirms and kicks as I lift him into the shopping cart seat at Quality Foods in Courtenay. Gerald, his dad, strides through the front doors, his black shirt unbuttoned; sparse, wiry white hair on his head and chest wave in the air like antennae. He's manic today. Nothing and no one can stop him. He grabs a handful of cherries, pops one into his mouth, doesn't even break his stride. A tanned, overdressed tourist stares at him. Her eyes dart from me to Ben to Gerald and back to me.

I give her a faint smile and try to catch up with Gerald as Ben squalls, tired and hungry as I am. No doubt she's thinking: *What's wrong with her? He's old enough to be her father.* But I don't have to explain anything. It's none of her damn business. Besides, she has no idea how much I don't want to be here, how soon I'll be gone once my plan for getting off the Island is in motion.

When I find Gerald, he munches organic cashews from the bulk bins, not even trying to be discreet. I have to stop him before he gets banned from this store, too. He's already banned from the Extra Foods in Comox.

. . .

A week earlier, we'd gone to Tofino for a little break, as Gerald put it. A break for him, maybe. For me and Ben, not so much. We'd rattled across the Island in his 1971 VW bus, stopped in Port Alberni for Gravol. The road was insanely hilly the rest of the way. Couldn't make it into the Green Point campground on Long Beach when we arrived—it's booked a year in advance by people all over the world who come for the west coast wild waves. Instead we stayed at a parking lot-like place down the road. Noisy, full of young surfers. Ben and I slept on the fold-out bed in the main part of the bus. Gerald stayed out late, scrounging beer and pot and I don't even want to know what else from the kids in the campground, and woke us up when he came back in the middle of the night to sleep in the pop-top above us.

We took Ben to Long Beach the first morning and he had a great time wading in the cool, misty surf, picking up shells and crabs and driftwood and seaweed. Gerald seemed good that day, calm and clear, and on his good days I could kind of understand what my sister Jenn once saw in him, maybe still saw in him. Sadly, his good days, from what I could see, were growing fewer and fewer.

"Let's drive into town and find some lunch, Liz," he said after a couple of hours. "I'll take Ben to the change room to with me."

Inside the ladies' change room on Long Beach, it's possibly even colder than it is outside. Across from me, three girls giggled uncontrollably as they tried to squeeze their goose-pimpled flesh into black surf wetsuits. They made eye contact and they broke into full-blown laughter, and after that it was hopeless. They might have been there for hours after I left, trying to get into their wetsuits, trying to stop laughing. Ladies, next time: wetsuits on first, then get high.

When I came out, I looked for Ben and Gerald in the parking lot and thought about how carefree those girls were. I could have been one of them once. How did I lose my freedom so suddenly?

Ben, of course. I love that little guy so much. Gerald turned out to be useless when it came to looking after him, so I felt like I had to stay for a while, at least until the business sold. It was starting to look like that would never happen, though. And in the meantime, I felt like life was passing me by.

. . .

Most nights after Ben and Gerald are asleep, I go online for a while. I keep in touch with Jenn during the week, tell her what to expect when she's back Friday night. I look for better jobs and, like my sister found out and like we both knew all along, most of the better positions are in Victoria or Nanaimo.

Once in a while there's a brief message from my friend Ryan. *Sorry I won't be able to make it over for a couple of weeks or so; you know how it is, Liz. :)* Lately, it's harder for me to take his little smiley faces seriously. I look at his Facebook profile, not just to see his handsome face but to see if I can figure out what it is that's keeping him so busy. He doesn't post very often, though. I suppose he really is busy.

Sometimes I look at his wife's profile, too, a different selfie every time. If I knew anything about ballet, I could tell you the name of the position she's in for her cover photo: up on one foot, the other leg almost straight up in the air, flashing a big grin for the camera. Only she's not a ballerina, she's a stockbroker, and she's not wearing tights or a tutu, she's wearing a t-shirt and Daisy Duke shorts, and the picture looks like it was taken in a bar. So it's none of my business, right? I'm not her employer, God knows. I don't even know her, though I feel like I do because I've heard so much about her. And like I say, I don't know anything about ballet. Or stockbroking. Or Brazilian waxes. But I know if I were her employer, I'd be having a little chat with her about professionalism.

Sometimes I think late night surfing is for the birds.

. . .

One of my jobs is working at the video store Gerald and Jenn
bought twelve years ago in the town strip mall. Well, both their
names are on the lease, but Jenn put up the money. Gerald has
no money, has never really held an actual job. My sister's crazy,
staying with him all these years. But it's her life. They bought
the store and Jenn quit her position with the government in
Victoria and they moved up island to Bowser, about forty minutes south of Comox. Things were fine for a while. At first, they
did well renting videos, and later DVDs, to the tourists. Then
Netflix came along. Now the store is dying. It all happened so
fast. A few years ago it was a thriving business: they even had
two part-time employees. It was hard to find internet access in
this area at all, then. Now it's everywhere and no one except seniors who haven't mastered Netflix yet want to rent DVDs. And
even they mostly borrow DVDs from the public library branch
a few doors down from us in the mall. Jenn and Gerald put
business up for sale three years ago.

After Ben was born, Jenn had to take another position with
the government in Victoria, Monday through Friday. Friday
night she's back late and Monday morning she's up at 4:30 to
make it to work in time. I quit my joe job at Superstore in
Nanaimo to come and look after Ben until they found a buyer
while Gerald ran the store. It was all supposed to be temporary and it was all supposed to be simple. We each had our roles
to play: Jenn making money in Victoria, Gerald running the
store, me looking after Ben. But there's a weak link: Gerald is
not capable of running a store. He is also not capable of looking
after Ben most of the time. So I look after Ben and I do a lot at
the store. The good or bad thing about it is that the store is not
what you would call busy at all, ever, anymore.

Gerald, like I said, is not capable of running a store, but
he has strong opinions about it all the same. Once when Jenn

was home, I'd again brought up the idea, over dinner, of just closing the store.

"We sell off the stock and the fixtures. And when the lease is up next year, we're done."

Jenn nodded. "I think so. Times have changed since we bought the place."

"If times have changed, we just have to change with them. We need to broaden our focus," Gerald insisted.

"How?" I asked.

"We bring in some other stuff. The movies aren't renting like they did before, but we can bring in more snack food. Local products for the tourists."

"There's already a grocery store in the mall. And a coffee shop," Jenn pointed out.

"So much negativity at this table. You're unwilling to try new things. Open your minds."

I'd known Gerald long enough to be able to read between the lines. *Do what I want. Do what I'm telling you to do.*

"Fine," said Jenn. "I'm tired. I don't want to spend my weekends here arguing."

. . .

As I put away the few DVDs from the return chute, I notice a thin stream of water running out under the backroom door, darkening the beige carpet. I set the pile of movies down, swing open the door and see a puddle flowing out from the bathroom.

"Ben!" I try the doorknob, but it's locked.

"Ben! What are you doing in there?"

"Just a minute."

"Open the door!"

He finally gets the door open and the toilet is overflowing, full of all the paper that used to be on the roll. His pants are soaked almost up to his knees.

"I'm sorry," he sobs.

"Oh, Ben!"

It takes all my self-control not to get mad at him. I start plunging and then the bell on the door rings. Of course.

"I'll be right out," I yell, hoping the customer hears me. After another thrust, the swirling slurry drains under the plunger. I wash my hands and step into the front, but whoever it was is already gone.

Where the fuck is Gerald? He was supposed to be here this morning, not me. I was supposed to take Ben to the beach. He said was just stepping out to buy cigarettes, would I mind waiting until he got back. That was over an hour ago.

"Come on, buddy," I say to Ben. "I'll take you home and get you cleaned up. Let's start this day over."

. . .

My other position is working for my friend Rhonda as a cleaner for vacation rental properties. Lots of owners in this area are from Victoria or Vancouver or Alberta. They rent these places online through VRBO, Vacation Rental by Owner, and Rhonda and I clean them in between rentals. That was how I met Ryan.

Rhonda called me to go clean a cabin in Buckley Bay, near the Denman Island Ferry terminal. She gave me the address and the combination for the door, and I packed my supplies in Jenn's ancient Dodge Charger and drove up. It was a nice place: big floor-to-ceiling windows facing the ocean. Two big bedrooms upstairs. A stone fireplace in the living room.

A black BMW sat in the gravel driveway. After I opened the door, I yelled "Hello" a couple of times. No answer, so I opened the windows and started with the kitchen sink and counters. Dusted, wiped off the leather furniture. I headed upstairs to change the bedding and towels and clean the bathroom before vacuuming and taking the garbage out.

As I rinsed out the bathtub, I sang, like I always do when I'm cleaning. "Blue skies…shining on me…"

"You have a lovely singing voice," said a man's voice, low, behind me.

I froze, couldn't breathe for a second. I swallowed and turned around slowly to face whatever awaited me. A tall man in plaid sleep shorts with mussed brown hair smiled at me.

"I'm sorry. I didn't realize you were here."

"I'm not supposed to be. Apparently I overslept."

"I can come back later."

"Don't worry about it. If I could just get in here for a minute."

"Of course."

I went downstairs to vacuum. In a few minutes he came down, dressed, on his phone. He caught my eye and winked before he went outside. I finished the bathroom, changed the bedding, vacuumed upstairs. He was sitting on the deck when I came to take the garbage out and load the laundry into the back of my car.

"Sorry again about disturbing you."

"No, it's okay. It's all my fault."

"Do you want me to lock up?"

"I don't know. Maybe. Turns out the meeting I'm missing isn't all that important after all."

"That's good. I guess."

"It does free me up for the rest of the day. So I was wondering if I could buy you lunch."

My immediate thought was *No. I can't.* But then, actually, why not? I wasn't busy the rest of the afternoon. Gerald had Ben.

"Lunch. Really? You don't even know my name."

"What's your name?"

"Liz. What's yours?"

"Ryan. Pleased to meet you. So, Liz. Can I buy you lunch?"

. . .

Before long, we sat in the breeze on the patio at the Fanny Bay Inn, sipped cold beer, ate barbequed salmon. What had got into me? I used to be more cautious than this, going out with some guy I'd just met. I knew nothing about him. He could be an axe murderer. He could be a squatter. A squatter with a new iPhone and a BMW 750i. Then I thought about the stoned girls in the change room at Long Beach. Would any of them hesitate for one second to go out for lunch with a handsome, apparently well-to-do gent? No way, baby.

"So, Ryan, you were saying you missed a meeting."

"Yeah. I should have been up at six and heading for the ferry in Nanaimo to be in my office in Vancouver at ten."

"What do you do?"

"I'm a lawyer," he said, glancing at his phone.

"So, you live in Vancouver?"

"Yes. We own a number of investment properties around the Island, though, and I came out here to get away for a few days."

"Your firm owns them?"

"My wife and I own them."

What was the right reaction to that piece of information, I wondered? "Oh."

"We're getting divorced. I'm out here to check on the properties so we can sell them. Dividing the assets can be complicated."

"That must be stressful."

"Well. It was a long time coming. Kara's a stockbroker, busy, busy, all the time. We hardly saw each other by the end. And when we did, it wasn't good anymore."

"That's a shame."

He shrugged. "That's life. But enough about me. Tell me about yourself."

"Well, you know I clean rental properties in the area. I also work at my sister's business, Lighthouse Video in Bowser."

"How's that?"

"Slow. Just like everything else around here."

Ryan laughed. His teeth were straight and white. "You got that right. It's like this whole island moves in slow motion. So are you going to keep working there?"

"God, no. It's only still open because my brother-in-law won't give up on it. I need to go back to school, do something with my life. Not sure what, yet."

"You could be a singer."

"Maybe. Whatever I do, it'll be off the Island."

"Good for you. UBC's a great school."

"I might apply there. But first I'll need to get a job."

"I'm sure you could find a position in Vancouver."

"Maybe."

"Maybe I could help you."

"Maybe you could."

"Can I see you tomorrow?"

"Maybe."

. . .

For a while, Ryan came out every weekend, which worked well because Jenn was home then. We met in a different place every time; he and his wife had properties scattered along the Old Island Highway and on the Gulf Islands.

We met up once at his place in Buckley Bay. "Your birthday's next week, right?"

"Yeah, Tuesday."

"Come see what I got you."

We got dressed and went out to the shed behind the cabin. Beside his two sea kayaks sat a third one, a new Jackson Journey, blue and white.

I threw my arms around his neck and kissed him. "Thank you. Wow, it's beautiful!"

"You want to try it out before the sun goes down?"

"Sure."

I'd kayaked lots before. Rented, used friends' kayaks. Ryan and I had kayaked together a few times and I'd used Kara's. But I never dreamed I'd have my own. We got into our kayaks and pushed away from shore, paddled around the bay a little until it got too dark.

My heart pounded all the way back to the cabin after we brought the kayaks in. Not from exertion, though. You figure a guy's serious when he buys you a sea kayak.

. . .

One Saturday morning at his condo in Parksville, I reached across a snoring Ryan to pick up my phone from the bedside table. It was Jenn.

"Hey, sorry to bother you. Gerald was charged with shoplifting at Quality Foods yesterday. We have to have a long talk this weekend."

"Good. Things need to change."

"They do. Okay, I'll see you later."

Ryan finally woke up. I could see how he'd overslept that first day we'd met. He seemed to be able to sleep through anything.

"Hey, babe. Who was that?"

"My sister. Gerald's been charged with shoplifting."

"He really is a fuck-up, isn't he?"

"Total fuck-up. He and Jenn will be having a little discussion today."

"Then you don't need to rush back."

. . .

"I was just about to have a glass of wine. Will you join me?" Jenn asked when I got back to their place later.

"Sure. How'd the talk go?"

"It took a while to work things out. Gerald's out cooling off. You know what he's like."

"Oh, yes. I do."

"So Ben and I will stay with my friend Margaret in Victoria for a while. We're putting this place up for sale. And Gerald will sell off the store stock and the fixtures, like we've said for a while. Then he'll come to Victoria."

"That could take a while."

"We'll come for visits. He says he'll get therapy."

"He's said that before."

"Yes. But Ben and I have to move on. There's more kids in Victoria. It'll be good for him."

"You're right"

"You can come with us if you want. But you have this boyfriend here now."

"Yeah."

. . .

Two days after Jenn and Ben go to Victoria, I finally get a late-night email from Ryan. This one has no emoticons of any kind.

> *Dear Liz,*
>
> *I wish I had a better way to say this, but I don't. Kara and I are reconciled. The divorce is off.*
>
> *I'll miss you so much. And I'm sorry to have to tell you in an email, but you know how it is. I won't be out to the Island again for a while. But I hope to see you again some time. I hope we can still be friends.*
>
> *xo Ryan*

. . .

My paddle slices through the calm waters of Buckley Bay, its splashing the only sound besides the screech of birds. I'll make it to Denman before dark. Ryan's cabin is only a couple of kilometers away and I have the combination for the door. I can kayak almost right up to it. I brought food, water, clothes, all the money I have, and my phone. I only plan to stay until I figure out what I'm doing next, but I have no wish to hang around with Gerald at my sister's place. He's been pretty growly since they left.

I think about finding a job in Vancouver. Of course, Vancouver is expensive, so I'll need a good job. With the kind of experience I have—retail, child care—that could be difficult. I figure that's where my *friend* Ryan comes in. Partner in a law firm? He can help me find a job. Hell, he could give me a job. He could even help me with going back to school. So much I could do if I can get off this island. I'm sure he'll be willing to help me. After all, he wouldn't want to put himself in an awkward position. There are some things Kara might not want to hear, right?

Soon I'm all set up in the cabin, showered, ready to relax. It's a nice place: big floor-to-ceiling windows facing the ocean. Two big bedrooms upstairs. A stone fireplace in the living room. Yeah, beats the hell out of the bedroom I had in Jenn and Gerald's little three-bedroom bungalow in Bowser. There's even a couple of bottles of wine stashed in a cupboard. I open one, pour myself a glass and settle down on the big leather couch across from the fireplace, watch the twinkling lights of the cruise ships gliding by. I already feel a lot more relaxed, clearer. I have a plan, now.

I raise my glass. *Here's to you, Ryan. I think this is the beginning of a beautiful friendship.*

NO ONE TO LOVE

January 3, 1903

Lately I've been moving more slowly than I used to. I've been feeling tired. The doctor laughed last month when I told him that. "Mrs. Wiley, you're seventy-three years old," he said. Funny, but until then, it hadn't occurred to me that I was getting elderly. Now that I think about it, though, I've worked my whole life. Not just for the Pennsylvania Railroad, either: I've taken care of two husbands, my daughter and my two grandchildren, my mother, my sister, and her five children. I guess I shouldn't be surprised at feeling tired. Then my granddaughter Jessie got it into her head to throw a grand party for forty guests here on New Year's Eve. I believe I'm still tired out from that.

And it's so cold this morning. I decide to sit down beside the hearth in the kitchen, pull the rocking chair closer to the fire. Soon my eyes close, my head begins to nod.

September 1860

Stephen's chin bobs in triplets, in time with the rhythm of the rails, rests sometimes on his chest, cushioned by the brown silk cravat that holds together the collar of the too-large shirt his brother Morrison sent him. Marion curls in the crook of her father's arm. Beautiful dreamers. They are so much alike: the same dark hair, the same gentle brown eyes, the same love of music. They nod together in three-quarter time, a nodding duet, and I have no wish to wake them. They are all I have in this world, and I suppose I am all they have, besides each other. Lord knows we have nothing else.

Rain splatters the window beside me, and I pull my shawl tighter around my shoulders. We are leaving Pennsylvania for New York, again. Stephen has talked me into it. I believe I never will know how it is he can talk me into things.

After we had been married three years, I took Marion, who was two, and went back to Mother, and he moved to New York. I told him I had had enough; we could not live on what he made writing songs. But I could not stay away from him for long, not even a year. I missed him too much. He haunted my dreams every night, and Marion kept asking for her Papa. So, six years ago, the two of us made this same train trip to join him. We lived in New York for a few months. I hated the boarding house we lived in: crowded, noisy, smelling at all times of cooked cabbage and slop buckets. And Marion and I missed Pittsburgh, missed our family, the McDowells and the Fosters both, and our friends. All the times we needed a hand, at home they were right there for us. I didn't realize until we moved how much we'd come to rely on our dear ones for so many things: for a meal, to look after Marion sometimes, for comfort and sympathy. In New York, we were strangers. Strangers in a big city full of strangers, people from all corners of the world speaking all kinds of languages, and so many much worse off than we.

When I protested this latest move, he said, "My dear, if anything the music publishers are even more centered in New York now than they were six years ago."

"Last time we moved to New York you said you'd make a go of it there. You said you'd be able to make a real living."

"We didn't stay long enough. That was the mistake. I wasn't there long enough to establish myself with the music publishing houses. I can't guarantee you an easy life from the beginning. But give me a chance."

"How many chances must I give you? We can't live on melodies, Stephen."

"You have my love for always, and so does Marion. Stay with me, let us be a family together. And the hard times will pass, you'll see. Besides, I'm done with blackface songs. My new pieces are in a far more genteel mode. They'll find a wider audience. You'll see, my love."

Marion opens her eyes, looks around for a moment as though she isn't sure where she is.

"Mama, is it time to eat yet?"

I smile at her and yet my jaw tightens a little. It's past noon and we have been on this train since early morning, and we last had a bowl of oatmeal when it was still dark. How can I tell her that I have three boiled eggs and three slices of rye bread and butter, and that will have to tide us over until we get to New York late this afternoon?

"What does my little miss want to eat?" asks Stephen, opening his eyes. "Would you like to go the dining car?"

"Oh, yes, Papa."

I give him a look as we make our way to the dining car. "Tut, tut. Don't worry yourself," he whispers.

One of Stephen's surprises. He has borrowed money from someone at home or sold the last suit Morrison gave him. Or perhaps he still has a bit of the $200 from Firth, Pond & Company. Last month he sold them all rights to the songs published under his prior contract with them for $1,600. But he owed them almost $1,400 in advances. He has a head for music, not for business.

I sigh, not too loudly. He's right, why worry? For now, we

will eat. Though part of me wonders if Stephen is more interested in the drinks he can get in the dining car than in eating.

October 1861

Marion and I don't last long in New York this time. Our boarding house is possibly worse than the one we had before. Stephen is writing fewer songs, and the ones he does write don't sell like the old ones did. Maybe he should have stuck to writing the blackface songs. The new ones are all about dead children, and dead lovers and dead dogs. So maudlin. True, "Gentle Annie" was very successful, but it was published seven years ago. At least "Oh, Susanna!" was lively. And it brought in some money. And while I suspect Mr. Christy and his Minstrels made far more money from "Old Folks at Home" than Stephen ever did, it continues to sell. His latest effort is called, "Why Have My Loved Ones Gone?"

Why, indeed? We are gone, my love, because we need to eat. We are gone because we need to have a home to live in, not a room we've rented in a building with people coming and going at all hours, not a fit place to raise a daughter at all. It does not mean we don't love you. We do, with all our hearts. But we cannot stay.

He stood in the doorway of the bedroom and tried to stop me as I packed a trunk. "I'll sell more songs this year, Jane. Don't leave again."

"If you want to sell more songs, you need to write them first. And if you want to be able to keep writing songs, you need to stay away from liquor."

"That's an awful thing to say." He hung his head and for just a moment I was ready to take my words back, to say I was sorry. Only for a brief moment, though.

"It is not an awful thing to say. It's just the awful truth. We can't live this way. I've told you that before. I've given you chances. Too many chances. Now I have to think of Marion."

"If you were thinking of Marion you wouldn't take her away from me."

"I'm taking her away from you because you can't support us. Your drinking is tearing this family apart."

This was the conversation we'd had how many times? Hundreds, I'm sure. I would confront him about his drinking; he would blame my impatience for driving him to drink. I would realize that there was no winning this argument, that the only reasonable thing to do was to leave him, to give Marion and myself a chance at a decent life.

And now, back in Pittsburgh, I have a real chance to support us. Mr. Andrew Carnegie, head of the Pennsylvania Railroad's Pittsburgh Division, has hired me as the Railroad's telegraph operator. He says that young women operators are more to be relied upon than young men. I am so excited and honoured to be given this position of responsibility. Maybe I can even help Stephen back onto his feet with the money I make. Perhaps we can be together again.

I think frequently about the night Stephen asked me to marry him. Eleven years ago, though it seems like a lifetime. He and my other suitor, Richard Cowan, the attorney, had both come to call on me. Mr. Cowan left at 10:30, the customary time for such visits to end. But Stephen lingered.

We stood together near the hearth. The logs crackled and popped as Stephen took my hand and held it fast with both of his.

"Jane. I see that I am not alone in my pursuit of you. And I don't wish to waste my time, so I must have your answer now. Will you have me or no?"

Sometimes I have wondered exactly what made me say yes so quickly and decisively. Perhaps his gentle way. But more, it was his eyes. I saw his brown eyes spark and flicker as they moved over my face, my auburn hair, and down my neckline. I felt myself drawn to the light in his eyes like a moth.

November 1862

Another cool and rainy fall day and I return from another visit with my husband in New York. He was working on a new song called "Why, No One to Love?" when I left. The man will yet drive me mad. Stephen, we all love you. I love you too much for my own good. And yet you can barely keep body and soul together. Morrison had paid my train fare and given me money and more clothes for his indigent brother, my beloved husband.

When I arrived at his boarding house in the Bowery, I was greeted by his landlady, a square, serious Irishwoman. "Are you Mrs. Foster?"

"Yes."

"I am Mrs. Connelly. Your husband is behind almost three months in his board."

I paid her what Stephen owed, and paid for the next three months in advance. Then I climbed the stairs to his third-floor room. My knock was not answered, so I let smyself in. Stephen was in bed, burning with fever.

"Hello, Jane. It's good to see you."

I got him some cool water to drink, a cool cloth for his head. He told me he wasn't hungry, but I went out to buy food and some coal for the small heater in his room. He didn't say so, but it looked as though there had been no fire in it for a long time.

Within two weeks, with a little care and a little wholesome food, my husband had recovered. He had regained his health; I had paid his debts. He felt so well, indeed, that he suggested we go and dine together to celebrate, in the restaurant in the St. Nicholas Hotel, a short walk away on Broadway.

"It's the beginning of a new era for me. I know it."

"Dinner will be so expensive there, Stephen."

"Then we'll have lunch. Surely we can afford that."

It wasn't the money that concerned me. I still had a fair sum left from what Morrison had given me. I was worried about his drinking.

"You won't drink too much, will you, and lose all the ground you've gained over the last two weeks?"

"Of course not. It's a new era, I told you."

He talked me into it against my better judgement. He was fine while we ate, sipping only red wine, and I thought maybe he had really changed. But after lunch he insisted on ordering a series of large brandies. Finally, over his protests, I paid the bill, and as we careened back toward the boarding house, his arm flung around my neck for support, snow began to fall. I wondered how he would survive the winter, a man who would allow his circumstances to dwindle to the point where he had no money to buy coal.

Soon he was back in his bed, sound asleep. I pulled the thin curtain across the window and sat on the chair beside the bed. As I brushed an unruly strand of his hair out of his closed eyes, I thought of their light. Other people don't see the light in his eyes; it must be a spectrum of light visible only to the heart. I saw it again at lunch today when he took my hand and thanked me for taking care of him. For a little while then I thought that we might once again love one another as man and wife. Perhaps I could convince him to move home and I could keep working while he wrote his songs. Marion could have her father back. But after the second brandy, I knew none of this could happen, no matter how much I wanted it to.

They sometimes say of a man lost to drink that he is drowning his sorrows. But Stephen has managed to drown all his joys, all that was good in his life. And long ago, he drowned the spark of love. The fire between us has been snuffed out, for good, I fear.

January 16, 1864
Henry, Stephen's other brother, has come to meet Morrison and me at the St. Nicholas Hotel. George Cooper, with whom

Stephen had lately been collaborating, had sent Morrison a telegram last week saying his brother was very sick in hospital, wished to see him, and, as always, needed money.

Morrison asked me to accompany him to New York, and of course I was glad to. As I finished packing a small, worn leather valise, he came to my door, a telegram in his hand. He said nothing at first.

"What is it?" I finally asked, dreading to know what I already felt to be true.

"Ah, Jane. It's too late. Stephen's died."

That was two days ago, and I have not yet cried. I'm not sure why. None of us are surprised at the news: this was the road Stephen had been heading down at least the last ten years, and quite possibly longer. Perhaps all his life. I have not cried, but I have felt like an automaton. I have gone about silently, doing what I must. Maybe it's Marion that's kept me from crying. Telling her was so hard. She loved her father so. She has been inconsolable, and perhaps I felt that if I broke down, too, there would be no coming back. We could not both fall apart.

And now Morrison takes me by the arm and the three of us walk down Broome Street, into the undertakers. I hear pounding in my ears as the gentleman speaks to Henry. I let Henry and Morrison do the talking. I cannot say anything. We go down a short hallway and through an open door and there is an iron casket. I look up at Morrison and he nods. I approach the casket, put my hand on it for a moment, and then without thinking, I fall to my knees. *Stephen.*

I stay there a long time. I do not pray; I do not weep. I know his body is within this box, but I know that his spirit, his spark, has departed.

Once I get up, the gentleman takes us into an office. There are papers to be signed, the hospital bill, which Morrison again takes care of. Inside a manila envelope are Stephen's belongings from the hospital: a small, worn leather purse; thirty-eight cents in pennies and scrip; and a scrap of paper with the words 'dear friends and gentle hearts' written on it in his hand.

I cannot hold the tears back any longer.

January 5, 1903

As Matthew Welsh sat down to a large brandy after dinner, a messenger came to the door with a telegram. He thought of his grandmother, who had worked as a telegraph operator, as he opened the envelope.

Western Union Telegram
TO: Mr. Matthew Wiley Welsh, Boston, Mass.

Very regretfully must inform you that our grandmother, Mrs. Jane McDowell Foster Wiley, perished in hospital Sat. night due to burns suffered in a fire that morning. Her clothing caught fire as she sat near the hearth and though I put the flames out, her injuries were too grave. Funeral is set for this Fri., Jan. 9th.

Your sister,
Mrs. Jessie Rose

THE QUALITY OF MERCY

I'm about to make a call in my office in the back of the store when a news story on the radio catches my attention. "Firefighters are at the scene of a three-alarm blaze in Victoria Park this morning," says the announcer. "The former boarding house has stood empty for decades as city council has stalled in deciding what to do with the historic building, one of the last examples of the Queen Anne style of Victorian architecture in Calgary."

I stare out my frost-whorled office window, shake my head. Another one gone. The countless rooming houses, cheap apartments and fleabag hotels lost—the Beveridge Block, the Calgarian Hotel, the York, the Empress, the Cecil and so many others—in Victoria Park, in Erlton, in Ramsay and Inglewood, in the East End of downtown. The East Village as it's now called. Some of them torn down, some of them burnt down—accidentally or possibly conveniently—to make way for condos, condos and more condos. The National Hotel in Inglewood got off easy—it's now home to a chichi hipster restaurant with a $75 steak on the menu. These old inner-city neighbourhoods are all shiny and new these days, with their character and their history rapidly disappearing. But what about all the unwanted people who lived in these unwanted buildings—the addicted, the marginalized, the aged. Where do they go? The condos that replaced their homes aren't affordable housing, not for people like them, anyway. Don't these people matter?

Maybe these people don't matter to the councilors or the developers, but they represent a large number of our customers, along with the many who can't or won't pay $200 for a pair of jeans. And we've had to move the Sisters of Mercy store several times, too, as downtown becomes more and more gentrified and the cost of leasing retail space keeps going up. When I started, we were at 10th Avenue and 1st St. SW, near the 11th Avenue ALCB store, the center of the world for some of our regulars. Then we had to move to 13th Avenue and 4th St. SW, the former site of the Parkside Continental, where Shelf Life Books is now. When the rent there started climbing, we moved out to 17th Ave. SE in Forest Lawn, where some of our displaced people have moved, too.

Then the phone rings. It's Magdalena, our new part-timer, who's doing a shift on the floor. "Julia, can you come out to the front for a minute?"

At the cash desk, Magdalena nods at the tanned lady with her freshly dyed Melania 'do. She wears a Canada Goose parka and clutches a garbage bag. "Are you the manager?" she asks.

"Yes, can I help you?"

"I want to make a donation, but your clerk won't give me a tax receipt."

"She can't. I know that's done at thrift stores in the US, but not here in Canada."

"These clothes were on consignment. They're good quality. The woman at the consignment store said I could donate them to a thrift store and get a receipt."

"I'm sorry, but she was mistaken. We can't give you a receipt."

She looks at Magdalena, looks at me, looks at her empty BMW idling in the loading zone outside our front door. She sighs, and her breath ruffles the guard hairs on the dead coyote tail that trims her hood. "Fine," she says. She dumps the bag on the counter and storms out.

"Thank you," I call after her.

I take her donation to the backroom. Whether something's for sale in a thrift store or a consignment store, if it doesn't sell, there's a reason. I doubt these clothes were on consignment. The sweaters are perfumey and one is badly shrunken; the jacket and pants are pilly with wear.

Now I can finally call Gail at CUPS, the Calgary Urban Project Society. I've been putting this call off, hoping I wouldn't have to make it.

"Gail, I'm calling about a client you sent over with a voucher for clothes and some housewares a couple of weeks ago. Rick Cochran is his name."

"Rick Cochran…hang on, let me get the file out. Oh, right, I remember him. Was there a problem when he was in the store?"

"No. Not really. The thing is, we started him out when he came in, showed him where things were and told him if he needed help, just to ask. But then we found his voucher on a shelf, and he was gone. I was wondering if you'd heard anything else from him."

"He hasn't been back in, no. He was supposed to be starting a new job, which is why he needed the clothes."

"I guess it's not really that strange that he left without his stuff. But I'm curious because he worked here a long time ago."

"Really?"

"Yes. He was here when I first started. Kind of funny. So I'm a little worried about him."

"That is funny. I will let you know if we hear from him at all."

What I don't tell Gail is that I'm pretty sure I scared him off. I didn't mean to. When he'd come up to the desk with his voucher on a busy Saturday afternoon, I didn't recognize him. He was thin, bearded, wore a tattered, threadbare hoodie and pants of an indistinguishable colour. He gave me his form, I read over the list of items he needed and pointed to where they were in the store. Then I noticed his name at the top.

"You're not the same Rick Cochran who used to work here, are you?"

"Well, yes. I am."

"Wow! It's been a long time. I'm Julia, remember?"

He hesitated, as though he were trying to recall. "Oh, Julia… right. How are you?"

"I'm good. Still here after all these years. Mavis and Noreen both retired a few years ago, and I'm the manager now. How are you?"

As soon as this question was out of my mouth, I regretted asking it. Clearly, he was not doing all that well, if he was in here on a voucher. He didn't answer at first and I couldn't help but notice the tremor in his hands when I gave the form back to him.

"I'm okay. I have a job interview next week and I need some things."

"That's great. Well, I'll let you get after them and just bring them up to the front when you're done."

"Sure. Thanks, Julia."

I forgot about him for a few minutes in the rush of Saturday cold snap customers buying up toques, scarves, jackets, sweaters, anything warm. Then I found his abandoned voucher when my floor shift was over.

. . .

Mavis and Noreen were manager and assistant manager—Rick used to call them 'The Sisters'—and Rick had been full-time for a year when I started, almost fifteen years ago.

"I haven't always been a paid employee," Rick told me once. "When I first came here, I was a fine option."

"What does that mean?"

"I got fined for driving under the influence. But I couldn't pay, so I had to do community service instead. Once my time on that program was up, Mavis and Noreen asked me to stay on."

He was a nice guy to work with, friendly enough, but quiet a lot of the time. After I'd been there a few months, he just disappeared. Noreen said he'd done it before, and she was sure he'd come back, but he never did. Mavis said with his dark hair and piercing blue eyes he reminded her of her favourite actor, Montgomery Clift. The poor guy hadn't looked much like Montgomery Clift that day, though. I hoped he was okay.

. . .

Reading the paper with my breakfast the next day, this headline jumps out at me: "Man Dead in Victoria Park Fire."

> The body of a man was found in the remains of the former boarding house on 12th Ave. SE that was destroyed by fire yesterday. It is speculated that the man may have broken into the house and started a fire to stay warm as the temperature plunged to -29 degrees. The investigation continues.

On the bus on the way to work I find myself thinking about the copy of *Hans Christian Andersen's Fairy Tales* I got for Christmas when I was a kid. I was haunted and horrified by some of the stories—"The Red Shoes," "The Little Mermaid" (nothing like the sanitized Disney cartoon pap most people know). And particularly "The Little Match Girl," about a little girl sent out to sell matches who strikes one after another in an attempt to stay warm on a frigid night. I know these days Andersen's stories are dismissed as Victorian melodrama. What people forget is that so-called melodrama—stark, miserable poverty—was the real state of life for many people in those days. It's still the real state of life for many more people than we believe or want to believe. And they're right here in Calgary, not in some far away country we don't have to think about. Hiding behind our veneer of stylish cynicism, we distract ourselves with our busy lives, our phones, Netflix. It's easy not to see people we don't want to see, even when we pass them on the street or ride the C-Train with them. It's even easier when we force them out of their neighbourhoods and we never have to see them or think about them.

. . .

Gail at CUPS calls me that morning. It's not unusual for us to talk a couple of times a week, so I think nothing of it. She mentions a couple of clients she's referring to us and then says, "So unfortunately I have some bad news."

"Oh?"

"Yes. I was just told that the man who died in that boarding house fire was Rick Cochran."

"What? How do you know it was him?"

"After I talked to you the other day, I called the employer we'd set up the interview with and it turns out Rick didn't ever show up for it. I called Alpha House, The Mustard Seed, The Salvation Army, The Drop-In Centre, and no one had seen him, so I called the police this morning. They said a positive identification has been made and the next of kin has already been notified. I imagine it'll be in the news soon. I wanted to tell you before you heard it on the radio or something."

I stare beyond the frost on my office window, lost for words. "This must be a shock," Gail offers.

I let out a sigh. "A shock? Not really, no. But it is terribly sad."

"Terribly sad. He seemed like a nice guy."

"He was nice. Troubled, of course."

"Of course."

After I get off the phone, shut my office door and cry. Then I go downstairs and find a bag of men's pants, start sizing and pricing, but the tears come back. *Goddammit, Rick. Goddammit.*

REFERENCE QUESTION

December 23rd is the last night that the library is open before Christmas, and I've put off going out to the desk to relieve Kath as long as I can. I've gone to the bathroom, read the new memos: do not leave valuables at the reference desks, lock all doors to non-public areas at all times. I bring out a fiction truck to weed. The old wooden truck has a wonky wheel, won't move straight.

Jennifer, the admin assistant, cuts in front of me and commandeers it out the workroom door. "You shouldn't be pushing these," she says, stowing it behind the reference desk for me.

"I'm fine. But thanks."

When I get there, Kath is ready to go. "We've been working on this question all afternoon. I think we're done with it, but we wanted see if any of you night staff might have an idea."

I read aloud, "'What poem is quoted on Mayor Murdoch's headstone?' Something about dreams and thoughts. That sounds straightforward. He was our first mayor, right?"

"He was. It sounds easy but look at all the sources we've checked. We can't find a picture of the headstone, and we don't even know if there is poetry on it. Anyway, don't worry too much about it. I think we should just refer them to the city cemeteries department. Phone them back if you want, or we can tomorrow. I gotta go. Merry Christmas, Kristin."

Susan, Kath's shift partner, hesitates to leave before her relief comes.

"Who's on with you tonight?"

"Barb Geist."

Susan raises an eyebrow. "Oh. Well, it's been pretty quiet."

"Yeah. And I just saw her go into the workroom. So you go ahead."

"All right. Have a good night. And Merry Christmas."

"Thanks. You too, Susan."

The phone rings; it's harder to reach every time I come in. The caller wants a definition. I find the word in the dictionary on the end of the desk, and as I finish the call, Barb makes her slow approach. It's clear from her expression that each step is painful. Her clothes hang loosely. Her white sweater looks like a baby blanket thrown over her shoulders, the matching cap sits crooked over her now-downy scalp. Her yellow-tinged skin is transparent, papery, crossed with fine blue and purple veins.

Barb is a sub, has no regular hours or benefits, which is why she has to keep working, she says. I wonder if it's more than that, though. I wonder if it's a way to hold on to her identity and all the parts of her life that are not about being a patient, not being sick. She eases into her chair and I notice how little room she takes up in it, think about how much I now take up in mine.

"Hey, Barb. Good to see you."

"You too, Kristin. You look different since I last saw you."

So do you, I think, but cannot say. "Yes, things are coming along."

"What's your due date?"

"February 10th. I'm back for a week after the holidays and then I'm on leave."

"Seems not so long ago I was on mat leave, and now my youngest is finished university. Good for you, though. Take all the time you can get."

"I'm sure I'll be busy. And how are you?"

"Well. I've been better. And I need you to help me with something tonight."

"Sure. What is it?"

She reaches into a deep pocket in her sweater, brings out three prescription bottles, and slips them under the ledge of the desk behind her phone. "I need to take the blue anti-nausea one at 7:30, and then a white one and a yellow one at 8:30. Could you help me remember? These pills are the only things that allow me to function at all anymore, and I have to take them on time." Barb was once intense, hurried, always working on several projects and questions at a time. Now her pacing is slow, her focus is narrow, one small thing at a time. That's more disturbing than the physical changes.

"Of course."

"We're quite a pair, you and me," she says with a dry cough. "I hope we have a quiet night." I return Barb's wistful smile, and without thinking about it, my hand goes to my belly. A lump forms in my throat as I consider the new life growing within me while her life ebbs away.

. . .

Barb works on the headstone poem question until her break in the workroom with Cara from Social Sciences. No need to rush back, I say. It is so quiet on the desk. Even our crossword puzzle lady, who calls several times each evening asking for 'The Dictionary Department, please', doesn't call. A few of the usual sleepers are scattered around the floor, one sits behind the index table near the desk. Some snore, sunken into chairs, slumped into study carrels. Some smell of alcohol, of clothes worn for

weeks on end, bodies unwashed for longer. We have pamphlets
we're supposed to hand out 'as needed' about where they can go
to have showers and do laundry. My philosophy with those guys
is live and let live. I figure as long as they don't bother anyone,
why not let them sleep?

Our little white-haired Harlequin man gets off the elevator.
He moves slowly, always wears jeans, a grey wool jacket, glasses,
a wedding band on his right hand. He picks a romance novel and
sits by the paperback spinners. He likes sweet romances, the ones
without sex. The book is open flat on his lap so no one can see
the cover, and he usually gets through the whole thing in an hour.
Then he actually borrows Zane Grey westerns or Patrick O'Brian
sea epics. I worry about him. Is he alone? Does he have a family?

A kick, flutter, flutter kick inside distracts me. Family. Dave
and I will have one soon. Sleep hasn't been good lately, so I think
about it a lot. I worry. Before I got pregnant, I thought I had
my life under control. But having a baby feels more and more
like losing control. All these things happening to my body. Will
the baby be healthy? What will we be like as parents? Maybe we
waited too long, maybe we're already too set in our ways. Maybe
we'll mess up this poor kid's life.

A tall middle-aged man with Givenchy glasses and a North
Face jacket and his teenage son in a Gucci hoodie get off the
elevator together and head for the desk. The man drops a piece
of paper on it in front of me with call numbers in Jane from the
third floor's handwriting. "We need some books on the French
Revolution," he says.

As we head to the 944s, he continues, "He has a paper to work
on over the holidays, but we're going to our condo in Whitefish
tomorrow, so we thought we'd better rent some books now."

"Good idea," I say. Is he trying to impress the tired pregnant
lady who has given up telling people that you borrow library
books, you don't rent them?

Of course, the books are on the very bottom shelf, where ideally there shouldn't be any books. These shelves shouldn't be so full. The whole library needs a good weeding, but who will do it? We lost two positions in the department this year. Will there even be a job for me to come back to?

"Your books are on the bottom shelf." I hand the dad the piece of paper, his face and the boy's both blank. I smile and put my hand on my belly for emphasis, point to the middle of the shelf with the toe of my shoe. "They're both 944.04, right there."

"Uh-huh," the dad says, not moving. Not only does he not understand or care that getting these books would be very difficult for me, he probably has no idea what those numbers mean. Clearly, he has no intention of getting them himself. I think about calling a support worker, but none are in tonight. And I can't ask Barb to do it.

I lower to an unsteady squat (my center of gravity moves every day) and hold on to the shelf gingerly for support—unlikely that it would tip, but you never know. I pull the books, carefully straighten up and hand them to the man, feeling slightly dizzy.

"Do we rent these from you?"

"No. Sign them out downstairs on your way out."

"Great," he says. He and his son rush unseeing past homeless sleepers and our lonely Harlequin man. The elevator comes and they're gone, without a look back or a word of thanks.

When I return, Barb isn't back yet, but there's no one at the desk and the phones are quiet. I put them on Do Not Disturb so I can go to the bathroom—there's no way I can wait, with Mark Spitz doing the butterfly on my bladder. When I come back, even the sleepers seem to be clearing out.

. . .

Barb and Cara are done break, and Cara says she'll stay with Barb while I take mine. I'm glad; I don't want to leave Barb alone, but I do want to have a break. Not that I've been working so hard, but everything seems to wear me out now. I'm tired at night, but I can't sleep for long. I nap three or four times a day. I would nap here in the workroom if I could get away with it.

I sip water, eat some of the sweet, crumbly shortbread that Jennifer left for us, even though it'll give me heartburn. I look at the pictures on the bulletin board over Jennifer's desk, of her husband and junior high age son and daughter in Florida last winter. They all look so relaxed. Is that how we'll look someday, Dave and me and our kid? Kids? Or will I still be tired, achy, bloated? Anxious, like I often seem to be these days? It's hard to see anything beyond pregnancy right now.

Then a line of verse, maybe a glimmer of the answer to the headstone question, breaks into my consciousness, but before I can grab a pen, it's gone. Damn. With some questions, the harder you try to find the answer, the more elusive it becomes, like trying to grasp water in your closed fist. Sometimes if you relax, let go, the answer comes in a sudden wave. But not always. I thought that was happening now, but it was just a tease.

. . .

After Cara leaves, I check the display on my phone. "Seven thirty, Barb."

"Thanks, Kristin. Time for the blue one." Her bony wisp of a hand shakes a little as she reaches behind her phone, finds nothing. "Did I put them put them behind your phone?"

I find paper clips, elastics, dust. No pills. "No. Did you put them back in your pocket?"

We check all around the desktop, the floor, in the drawers. Barb checks in the workroom, in her purse, her coat pockets. I begin to feel sick. All three of Barb's medication bottles are gone. Stolen.

"I'm so sorry. It must have happened when I was in the stacks with a customer. And then I went to the bathroom."

"It's not your fault. Don't worry about it."

I pick up my phone. "I'm going to call security."

She shakes her head. "Why? They can't pat down everybody on their way out. Whoever has them is probably long gone, anyway."

"But you need those pills."

"I'll call Peter. He can drop by the pharmacy before he picks me up."

"Won't that mess up your schedule though?"

"Nah. I won't die," she says, and laughs. "Well, I mean, I will, but not from missing a couple of pills."

Hot tears sting my eyes. These days it seems like they're always just below the surface. "Why would they take your anti-nausea pills?"

"They probably didn't look at the label, just grabbed them and ran. You'd have to be pretty desperate to steal a cancer patient's drugs, but we both know a lot of desperate people come in here all day, every day. I shouldn't have left them out here, but I didn't want to forget to take them. Anyway, it's no big deal. I'll call Peter now."

I go back to weeding my fiction—yes, let's discard seventeen of this Danielle Steel title now—as Barb calls her husband. She is much calmer than I am about it.

"There," Barb says. "He's on his way to the pharmacy now and he'll come straight here. I'll be drugged up again in no time."

"That's good. Will you be okay until he gets here?"

"I will." But her face now has a greenish tinge. She takes a long, raspy breath before she says, "And Kristin—losing those pills is the least of my problems."

My tears escape. "Oh, Barb. Why would someone do this?"

"Who knows why? After working here thirty years, I can tell you this: not every question has an answer."

Frustration rises in me. "Maybe not every question has an answer. But does that mean we shouldn't look for it before we give up?"

Then the phone rings, someone from a branch wanting a shelf check. Conversations on the reference desk, even on quiet nights, are fragmented.

It's almost closing time when Peter Geist arrives. After visiting the washroom yet again I do the final walk around the floor while Barb switches off the computers and phones. We get our coats and purses, turn off the lights and take the elevator downstairs. Snowflakes catch in the lacy yarn loops of Barb's cap when we leave the building.

"Goodnight, Kristin," Barb says. "Merry Christmas."

I hug her carefully. She's like a dry leaf in my arms. "Merry Christmas to you both. Will I see you again after the holidays?" I look at Barb in the dim December light. More than ever now I see how frail she is, barely there.

"I don't know. But if I don't, enjoy that baby of yours. Okay? And you take care of yourself."

"I will, Barb. You, too."

As I walk to my car, I realize that the question I just asked Barb is one that does have an answer. I wish it didn't.

GLORY B

I kneel in the front yard planting tulip bulbs when my upstairs neighbour Glory comes out the front door, wearing dark glasses and a black coat, a fuchsia feathered and sequined clip that pulls her pink hair into a halo, and a big red purse slung over her shoulder. I hardly ever see her during the day, but I hear her and her friends until very late; sometimes I worry that they're going to set this old wooden frame house on fire. But this morning she's quiet, says, "Hi, Ruth," when she sees me, her front teeth smeared with orange lipstick. She doesn't stop to chat.

. . .

One day a few months earlier, on a Saturday afternoon after I got home from work, Glory had come downstairs to introduce herself, screw top bottle of rosé in her hand. The wine, I couldn't help noticing, was almost the same pinky colour as her hair.

"Glory's just my stage name," she'd said after I told her a little about my job at a bookstore a few blocks away. "My real name's Jean Bettelheim. Glory B's got a nicer ring to it, don't you think?"

After our laughter subsided, I asked her, "You have a stage name? Are you an actress?"

She refilled both our glasses. "Nope. Not yet. Right now I'm a dancer."

"A dancer? Ballet?"

"No. I'm an exotic dancer."

"Oh. That must be interesting." I couldn't think of anything else to say. I wondered what she'd told Dorothy, our landlady, about her job. I'm sure Dorothy wouldn't have rented the apartment to an exotic dancer.

Glory laughed again. "That's a good word for it, kid. Interesting. Although you'd be surprised at how routine the whole thing can get. I guess it's like any other job: some things about it you love. Some things bring you to tears. It's a living."

. . .

The next morning, I was really tired. Not so much from hanging around with Glory in the afternoon: we'd drunk the bottle of wine and she'd left. It was much later that things went bad. I'd gone to bed about 11:00. A banging on my bedroom window woke me up at 2:46. I heard a man's deep, raspy voice outside.

"Glory! Goddammit! I know you're in there! Open the door!"

I was about to open the window and tell him he had the wrong apartment, Glory lived upstairs, but by the time I got out of bed, he'd run to the front door. I stood in the dark hallway with my hand on the phone and watched him, backlit by a streetlight, through the sheer curtains on the front door. He was a big man. A big, angry man. Cursing and pounding on my door and windows. Sooner or later he'd break one of them, and then who knew what would happen? I picked up the phone and punched in '9'. Just as I was about to punch in '1-1', Glory opened the door to her apartment. I hung up the phone and went back to bed, my heart almost beating out of my chest.

I was afraid of what this man might do to Glory. I heard some shuffling, the creaking sounds of feet on the wooden floor above my head. Then music, talking, laughter. It didn't sound like she was in danger, or not anymore, anyway. Just as it started to get light, I drifted off to sleep.

The next morning—well, closer to afternoon—Glory was at my front door. "Ruth, I'm sorry about last night. Sorry about Garry."

"Garry? That's who was banging on my windows in the middle of the night?"

"Yeah. He's an old flame. But we lost our passion a long time ago. We met when I was dancing in Tuktoyaktuk."

"That must have been cold."

"Well, I was dancing inside a bar. Anyway, I didn't think he'd ever find me here. But he did. Sorry, it won't happen again."

. . .

All day I couldn't stop thinking about what had happened the night before with Garry and Glory. What was that kind of hot-blooded love like? Exhilarating, terrifying? Was it true that love made the world go around? Thinking about my own sorry non-existent love life was truly depressing now, if it hadn't been so before.

. . .

That night Glory was sitting on the front steps when I came back from getting some groceries. She wore sunglasses, even though the sun had already gone down.

"Hey, Ruth. I was wondering if you'd want to come up and hang out for a while after I get back from work tonight. I feel so bad about keeping you up last night."

"Yeah, I don't know. I'm pretty tired. What time do you get home?"

"Usually between 1:30 and 2:00. Why don't you have a little rest for a few hours and then come on up? I'll bring some wine from work."

"Between 1:30 and 2:00? I'll be asleep."

"But what if you have a nap now?"

"Glory, I have a job. I have to get up in the morning. And I don't appreciate being woken up in the middle of the night."

"Another time?"

"Maybe another time. But tonight, I need to get some sleep."

"Sure, Ruth, I understand. And I'm sorry."

I felt a sharp twinge as I watched Glory walk down the front sidewalk. I liked her, and I didn't want her to think that I didn't. But she needed to know that this kind of thing could not continue. She needed to know that she couldn't just walk into my life and mess it up.

. . .

Later I sat on the couch trying to read an anthology of earnest Canadian short stories, but I kept nodding off. When I gave up trying to read, I fell asleep right away, and soon I dreamt that I was in the club where Glory worked, the lone woman in the audience. I waited and waited for her to come on stage and drank big fishbowl glasses of blue and green and orange strange and sweet drinks while the other dancers went through their acts glassy-eyed and dull. Finally, Glory strutted onto the stage in a red sequined leotard with little red horns in her teased pink hair, a long red tail and a sparkly red pitchfork. The slinky curtain behind her was a wall of orange lamé flames.

"Good evening," she purred over the slick recorded dance music, scanning the audience with a gleam in her eye. "My name is Glory B. And I see my neighbour, Ruth, is in the audience tonight. How about coming up here and giving me a hand with the act, Ruthy?"

The audience clapped and stomped and whistled, but I was rooted to the spot. I wanted to speak but could not make a sound.

"Got a little stage fright, kid? That's okay. You're damned if you do and you're damned if you don't. The bouncer will help you up onto the stage. Garry, a little help here?"

Next thing I knew, I was sitting straight up on the couch in my dark living room, covered in sweat, heart pounding.

. . .

A week after the last time I saw Glory, our landlady knocked on my door. When I opened it, I could see she was upset; her face was white and her hands shook as she fidgeted with her keys.

"Is something wrong, Dorothy?"

"Do you know what happened to that librarian from upstairs?"

"Librarian? You mean Glory? I haven't seen her since last week."

"She told me her name was Jean. Come and see her apartment."

We climbed the stairs together and I peered in the open door. The middle of the living room floor was black and scorched, the cold wind blowing through the broken window still smelled of burn, even though the fire was long out. The furniture was mostly grey with smoke residue, and Glory's stuff looked to be all gone.

"Oh, my God," I whispered.

"I'll have to call the police. And the insurance," Dorothy said, shaking her head. "Some people."

. . .

Later I found a single fuchsia feather with purple sequins glued to it on the stairs and stuck it to my fridge with a magnet. Once in a while when I see it, I walk to the wine store and buy a bottle of rosé. But just once in a while.

LOVE STORY

I realized a while ago that Jack and I have lived in Glovertown a long time now. The change seemed like a good idea at first, getting away from the megapolis, the grind, the corporate world, and into a different way of life. But now I worry that we're stagnating. And I worry that some things never change.

One day as I weeded the garden, Jack came out of the house, cast a long shadow on my row of carrot seedlings.

"Sandra. I want to talk to you," he said.

I said nothing, dug small thistles.

"Sandra," he said again. "I want to talk to you."

I put my trowel down. "You want to talk to me? You want to talk to me? Where the hell were you last night? I wanted to talk to you then."

"I told you. I was at Safeway."

"What were you doing at Safeway again? We have plenty of food right here."

He shaded his eyes with one hand, looked out toward the road. "Man cannot live on vegetables alone."

. . .

The next morning, I awoke earlier than usual. I was surprised to find Jack in the kitchen, dressed, drinking coffee, staring out the window past the basket of violet petunias with a strange look on his face I had never seen before. He turned to me.

"Sandra, I think we've lost our passion."

"Passion? What does that even mean?"

"It means a zest for living. It means enthusiasm. It means a grand purpose."

What was all this about with Jack lately, anyway, I wondered. Then I started to wonder if we were still in love. There was a bond between us still, thicker than blood, and it had always seemed to be there. But now it didn't seem as important as it once did.

. . .

That night Jack came in late and drunk, his beard disheveled. He got into bed with me, but I said nothing, did nothing, just felt his cold feet on mine, smelled his brewery breath in my face.

"Sandra. I want to talk."

I said nothing.

"Sandra. I want to talk."

"If you wanted to talk, why did you go out and get drunk?"

"I needed to get brave first."

What was I supposed to say to that? You should have got brave years ago?

. . .

Later, I dreamt that I was late for a meeting. I couldn't find a place to park, I'd lost my briefcase, I drove to the wrong building. I woke up and realized the dream was really about Jack. Love is so weird, it's so hard to understand. But we're all supposed to just get it.

. . .

A week later, so much had happened. Jack had moved out. Then I saw him outside the library with that chatty cashier from the Safeway. They were talking up a storm, they couldn't stop talking, it looked like. I would have thought maybe he was happy, but he had that same strange look on his face I'd never seen before.

DEL

Layla tries to slice a tomato for the Denver sandwich that Bill Jensen, the new store manager, waits for as he talks and laughs in the lineup with some of the other department managers. She's new, still nervous. And she's so slow, makes the slices too thick, lopsided. Hasn't even cored it. I can't stand watching her.

"Don't you know how to core a tomato?" I half-whisper. I grab the knife from her and take a fresh tomato from the bin, slide the tip of the knife at an angle into the flesh at the top and twist the core out. She looks at me, says nothing, a long brown curl from her permed mop escaping from her hairnet. Has she heard me? Does she understand what I said? I can't tell.

Later in the break room, I wait for Bill to say something about the idiot girl who served him, but he doesn't. He chats and laughs and jokes with all of us, and before I know it, I'm fifteen minutes late going back.

Why does Human Resources hire these green kids to work in the cafeteria? I wonder as I fix my hair and lipstick in the bathroom. None of them know anything about food or cooking. Layla didn't even know how to make a grilled cheese when she started. Sixteen years old. When I was her age, I was driving the tractor and cooking for my dad's farmhands. By myself, after my poor sister Ruby died. Hell, I was married the year after that. Layla's in high school, says she wants to go to art college when she graduates. Jesus. She has these two girlfriends who come in and hang around talking to her at night. Don't think I don't see them. Look like shoplifters, the both of them.

The big shipment of produce I've been expecting was finally delivered while I was on my break. It was supposed to arrive this morning when I had more staff on, but now the two of us will have to unpack it all between customers before the store closes tonight. Just as Layla comes into the back for some eggs, I open a crate of strawberries and inhale their sweet, heady perfume. She starts a little when she sees me, and something in the way she looks, something about her eyes, puts me in mind of Ruby. Maybe I've been too hard on her. This is her first job, after all.

"Come here," I say. She looks a little unsure, maybe a little afraid she's done something wrong again, but comes over.

"Have a couple. They're delicious," I tell her.

She pops a big strawberry into her mouth, takes a bite, wipes the dribbling juice from her chin. "They are good. Thanks, Del."

The counter bell rings out front and she turns to go, but not before she takes another strawberry. First time I've ever seen that kid smile.

CHICKEN

"See? It's easy," Shannon panted, out of breath from running back into the shadows behind the bus stop. "Why don't you try it, chicken?"

"It's stupid," I said.

"It's fun. It's a rush. Why are you such a suck?"

"Fine."

I waited until I saw headlights come over the horizon and darted into the middle of the road. I stood there for a few seconds as the headlights got closer. My pulse pounded in my ears. I broke out into a cold sweat, ran as fast as I could back to the sidewalk. Shannon caught me in her arms and tried to push me back into the road, but I pushed past her and skidded onto the frost-covered grass, gasping.

"Oh my god, Kate. You're such a fucking baby! That car was a million miles away. Let me show you how it's done."

. . .

Earlier that night, the clerk at the downtown Bay cosmetics counter talked on the phone the whole time we were there. She glanced over and sized us up; clearly, we weren't rich old ladies there to buy Clinique or Shisedo, we were a couple of bored kids killing time trying on lipstick and perfume. She returned to her call while Shannon expertly ringed her mouth with the Lancôme lip liner tester and then filled in with Rose Absolu lipstick, pouted at her dark-haired, green-eyed reflection in the mirror on the counter for a long time.

Once my mom had said, "I like that Shannon. She's so pretty." That remark puzzled me at first, but later I realized that was Shannon's whole stock in trade, that she got away with things others never could have because of her looks. Only Shannon didn't know there was a limit to what even she could get away with.

Then, over in accessories, we tried on toques, found two we liked, checked ourselves out in the abundant mirrors. "Okay, we're done," Shannon said, the pom-pom on her silvery toque bouncing as she strode to the escalators. "C'mon, let's get out of here."

Always when we'd taken things before—makeup, jewellery, cigarettes—this was how it worked. It was never premeditated; Shannon would just suddenly decide we were shoplifting. I wouldn't have admitted it then, but she was the leader and I was the follower. And I'm not saying all the stupid stuff Shannon and I did was her idea, but a lot of it was. Then again, I didn't have to go along with it. But I did.

We took the escalator to the main floor in silence, our eyes darting around for any sign that someone had noticed us and our unpaid-for toques. My heart pounded as we made for the main doors and I winced, thinking surely an alarm would go off, or that someone would grab us. We stepped out the door and walked in brisk silence for another block. Adrenalin-shot, I looked back, expected to see a security guard or a cop behind us. Nothing. Just early Christmas shoppers, grey businesspeople finally leaving overtime.

"See? Easy. Now we go to the liquor store," Shannon declared.

"What if they ID us?"

"It'll be fine. We both look older; we're wearing lots of makeup. They'll never even ask."

A man almost my dad's age was stocking the shelves in the liquor store across the street from the Bay and he came over to us right away. I thought the jig was up, that he was going to ID us and kick us out.

"Something I can help you ladies with?"

"Oh, I think we'll be all right, thanks," Shannon said, and smiled at him.

I might as well not have been there. His eyes were fixed on Shannon's lovely face. "Well, you just let me know if you have any questions," he said, and went back to his boxes. If I had come in alone, he would have kicked me out. Shannon, though, could take chances and risks that normal people would never dare to.

We selected a mickey of tequila from the rows of sleek bottles. The bored salesclerk, also on the phone the whole time, paid no attention to us, just took our money and gave us our bottle in a brown paper bag.

We walked a little way to a bus stop and sat down on the bench. Even in the cold, the inside of it smelled like stale garbage and cigarette butts and piss. Shannon took the mickey out of the bag, unscrewed the top and handed it to me.

"See, Kate? Once again—easy. Bottoms up."

I held the bottle up to my nose. It smelled like turpentine. I handed it back to her.

"You first," I said, my cloud of frozen breath hanging in the air between us. She put it to her lips and guzzled half the bottle.

"There you go," she said, handing it back to me.

I did it the same way she did, poured the foul liquid down my throat until the bottle was empty. A warm feeling started to creep up from my toes.

"Okay. We drank it. What should we do now?" I asked.

Shannon got up, pulled me by the arm and dragged me behind the bus stop, where we slipped a little on a patch of ice in the shadows. "I know," she said. "Let's play Chicken."

"What's Chicken?"

"What's Chicken?" She howled with laughter. "Fuck me! You don't even know what Chicken is?"

"No. I don't. What is it?"

"Watch. I'll show you." She waited until she saw a car coming and ran out in front of it.

"Shannon!" I screamed. "Oh, Jesus!"

But she ran back just in time. And then I tried it. And she decided to take another turn, to show me how it was done.

Another pair of headlights came over the rise, moving faster than the first car. "Watch. I'm not afraid," Shannon said, and ran out into the middle of the road, stood with her arms and legs starfished open.

A gust of wind blew some dry leaves into her face, but she did not flinch. I held my breath: the car swerved and skidded on some ice. It all happened so fast that even now I am not absolutely certain if she had started moving at the last minute, or couldn't move, or just wouldn't. But the car squealed to a stop after smashing through the bus shelter's front window. From behind the shelter, I saw Shannon crumpled against the curb, face down on the pavement in a widening red pool. I knelt on the ground beside her.

"Shannon!" I screamed and shook her shoulder. She didn't answer or move. "Oh, Jesus! Shannon!"

A man got out of the car. "What the hell are you—oh, Jesus," he said, when he saw Shannon. "I'll call 911."

It was probably only a few minutes until the police and the ambulance got there, but it seemed like forever. I kept shaking Shannon's shoulder, wondered if I should try to move her, fought off the urge to throw up. Soon flashing lights surrounded us, a policeman pulled me away from Shannon and started asking questions I was mostly too stunned to answer. I didn't really want to watch and yet I could not tear my eyes away as they eased her up from the curb and onto a stretcher. Her bloody, broken face was misshapen, nose flattened into a pulpy mass. I couldn't tell what was flesh, what was gravel, what was bone. The toque she had just shoplifted was blood soaked, a few still-dry strands of pom-pom wavering momentarily in the breeze before they slid her into the back of the ambulance.

After that, I threw up.

. . .

The next thing I knew I was in a hospital bed. I opened my eyes and my dad sat in a chair next to my bed, his chin resting on his chest, small puffs of snore burbling from his lips. Once I realized where we were, and why, I started to cry.

"Kate?"

"Yes, Dad," I sobbed.

"How are you?"

"I'm okay, I guess. Nothing really happened to me. But."

I was about to ask him about Shannon when I heard a piercing cry of pain, like an animal, in the hall outside my room. I saw Shannon's mom, her face in her hands, being led down the hall past my room by a nurse.

I swallowed and looked back at my dad. He didn't say anything. He didn't have to.

BROWNTOWN

The last time I saw Janet, she called me out of the blue one morning. I hadn't heard a peep from her in over a year. "I didn't know you were coming home for Christmas," I said, cradling the phone with my shoulder while I washed my breakfast dishes. "Where are you? I can hardly hear you."

"I'm at Deerfoot Mall right now. And I didn't actually come home for Christmas."

"Oh no? I mean, it is Christmas in a week and a half."

"Yeah. It's a long story, Charlotte."

"Okay." It was always and ever a long story with Janet. I would have expected nothing else.

"So, I'm going back today. Could you drive me to the airport?"

"Uh." Even though it was my day off, I scrabbled in my mind for some excuse, some reason that I could not. Nothing came. Fuck.

"Charlotte?"

"Yeah, I guess I can. When's your flight?"

"4:00. If you come get me now we can have lunch and I can tell you all about it."

I took a deep breath, let it out. "Yeah, okay."

. . .

The sun slanted low through my cracked windshield on the long trek to Deerfoot Mall. The week-long snow-eating chinook wind had taken Calgary, as it often does, from winter wonderland to Browntown, with only patches of dirty grey ice left lurking in shadows. My rusted smoke-belching Chevy Nova was almost out of windshield washer fluid, and I had almost a quarter tank of gas.

I cursed myself for being unable to say no to her. Janet had sat behind me in junior high, copied my answers on tests, asked me what I got for this question or that one. We got to be fairly close eventually. But she hit the road after high school, drifted back and forth from Vancouver to Victoria, and up and down the Island and the Lower Mainland: Nanaimo, Powell River, Abbotsford, Surrey. The only time she ever got in touch with me was when she wanted something, usually a ride, since I had nothing else to give her. She knew I had no money. But she was always happy to bum a ride, some weed, a place to crash, usually out of the blue, always on her own terms, never with any thought of how she might be inconveniencing me.

Normally I try not to get anywhere near a mall in December. Even though I ended up having to park on the outer periphery of the parking lot, I made it to the crowded food court at 12 o'clock, as we'd agreed. A mom with her two little kids was just leaving and I snagged their table, wiped the juice and salt off it, knocked the stray french fries onto the floor. Knowing Janet, I was not at all surprised when she wasn't there, or when it took her almost another hour to show up. I was just about to go back home, thinking I was off the hook and could chalk up the gas money to experience, when she finally showed up.

Her brown hair was pulled back in a tight ponytail, her jeans and dingy grey sweater needed washing. She dumped an armful of shopping bags on the floor beside the table, pulled her duct-taped carry-on bag closer, and sat down. "Just thought I'd do some Christmas shopping while I was waiting."

You've been waiting, I thought. Before I could respond, she eyed my hair. "Is that a new colour?"

"Yeah, I think it's a little different since the last time I saw you."

"It's very vivid."

"Thanks. I guess. Sorry, I already ate." *I already ate because I knew you'd be late, like you always are.*

"We were going to meet at 12:30, right?"

I sighed inwardly. "We said 12. And it's almost 1 now. That's okay, you go ahead and get something, and I'll watch your stuff."

She frowned, annoyed, and started to get up, then sat down again, licked her lips. "I'll just eat on the plane."

"Are you sure?"

"The thing is, I spent all my cash."

I looked at the bags of gifts around her feet and looked her in the eye for a moment before I said anything else. "I can buy you some lunch, if that's what you're getting at."

"What? No! I just mean, you know, I don't have any cash. But if you don't mind, I can buy you some lunch the next time you're out my way." Classic Janet. Classic. She'd pulled that one on me almost as many times as her other favourite ploy: "Oh, I forgot my wallet." Such bullshit. I have never once forgotten my wallet.

Luckily, I had been paid the day before. I got my wallet out of my purse and gave her a twenty.

She returned with a burger, fries and shake on a tray. "Here's your change," she said, and gave me a handful of wadded-up bills and coins the way you'd expect a six-year-old to.

"I'm going to get a coffee," I said. "Do you want one?"

"No, I'm good."

I returned a few minutes later, set my coffee on the table and put what was left of the wad of change in my jeans pocket before I sat down. "So, how are you?" What brings you home before Christmas, but not for Christmas?"

"I came back to have an abortion on Tuesday."

"Oh. I—I'm sorry."

"Don't be sorry. It wasn't a big deal."

"Why did you come home for it, though? Couldn't you have had one in Vancouver?"

"I was able to get into the clinic here faster. And then I stayed with Mom and Dad for a couple of days to rest."

I winced. Janet's dad was a drinker with a quick temper, and she always seemed to get on the wrong side of him. "So, what did they think about it?"

"Well, I wasn't going to tell them at first. I mean, they paid for my airfare when I told them it was knee surgery. Figured what they didn't know wouldn't hurt them. You know, with them being Catholic and all. I took the bus to the clinic, but I didn't really think about needing a ride back. When Dad came to pick me up there, the jig was pretty much up. He wasn't very happy about it."

"Awkward."

"Yeah. He hasn't said much to me since then, and when I asked him to take me to the airport, he refused. So I decided to take transit up here and grab Jason a few presents before I headed up to the airport."

"Jason's your new guy, I assume?"

"Yeah. He's a doll."

"Is he…did he know about the abortion?"

"No. I told him I was visiting Mom and Dad for a few days. He doesn't need to know."

If it had been anyone else, I would have asked her why he didn't need to know. Why he didn't come with her. But I knew Janet's veneer to be thin, and if you prodded it much, she was liable to lash out at you. There was no point in setting her off.

. . .

Clouds had moved in while we were in the mall, and I noticed the temperature had fallen a few degrees as we made our way, laden with Janet's shopping, to my car. We loaded her bags into the trunk of the Nova and pulled out onto Deerfoot to go to the airport.

Janet took a long drag from her cigarette, cracked her window down, and flicked the ash out. "This place is so boring," she said, looking from side to side. "So brown. I don't know how you can even stand it. Vancouver is still all green. There are even flowers out there."

"Yeah. Nice." I turned up the music on the radio, hoping she'd take the hint. I'd heard her 'boring Calgary' rant so many times before. And did not ask why, if it was so great on the coast, did she move every few months? Or why did she have to come home for a medical procedure? Again, there was no point in arguing with her and I wasn't up for it. This was almost over. A few more minutes and we'd be at the airport.

I pulled in to a just-vacated parking spot at the Arrivals door and helped Janet get her bags out of the trunk.

"Have a good flight."

"I will. Well, Merry Christmas, Charlotte."

"Same to you. Nice to see you."

"Yeah, you, too."

She slipped through the automatic door with all her bags and disappeared.

. . .

The drive home was pretty quiet. I'd beat rush hour by a good forty minutes. Just as I pulled onto my street it started to snow, small, dry flakes. Maybe we wouldn't have a brown Christmas after all. I brought in the mail—all bills—and checked the answering machine for messages. Before I put my purse away in the bedroom, I got my wallet out to put the change I had put in my pocket into the zipper section. As soon as I opened it, of course, I noticed that all the cash was missing. Cleaned out. She must have done it, I realized, when I was getting my coffee. It wasn't really that much, only about eighty bucks. But still. Merry fucking Christmas to you, too, Janet. You're welcome for the ride.

IN A MIST

January 1955

The music on the kitchen radio grows fainter as I carry the last box of Christmas decorations downstairs. Dust motes float in the beam of sunlight slanting through the basement window that leads my eye to the wooden crate on the bottom shelf. For a moment I wonder if my husband, Max, and I had overlooked a box of ornaments, but it all comes rushing back to me when I pull it out and see my name on the dusty label, in neat, precise script: *Miss Alice Weiss, #207 83 - 47th St., New York City*

The heavy crate had arrived at my apartment twenty-four years earlier. It held maybe a hundred records. Inside a large yellow manila envelope that smelled with damp and age was the portrait Bix had sent to his parents when he wrote to them about our engagement. In it, I am the very model of a modern It Girl flapper, bee-stung lips and curly red hair cut to look like my idol, Clara Bow. Bix called my hair colour Clarinet Marmalade. There were also some newspaper clippings, and a letter. I remembered bursting into tears the first time I'd read it:

December 15, 1931
Davenport, Iowa

Dear Miss Weiss,

Hoping this finds you well. My parents and I thought
you might want some of Bix's things. The envelope contains
a few articles about him that appeared in the Davenport
Daily Democrat. The records are Bix's own. He sent them
along to us as he recorded them.

Regards,
Mary Louise Shoemaker (née Beiderbecke)

I pick out a few of the 78's to put on the hi-fi upstairs while I
put on a pot of coffee: "Rhythm King," "Somebody Stole My Gal,"
"Davenport Blues," and "Sorry." Jazz critics and historians (how
Bix would have laughed at the idea of a 'jazz historian') now say
the box was a myth; that Bix's parents played and loved all the records. Some say Bix gave me his piano. Not true, I don't know what
became of that. Others say that I was a myth. How can something
that happened just twenty years ago be already lost in the mists
of time? Maybe Bix would have wanted it that way. Let them say
what they want, though—what people think doesn't matter to me.

I know what Bix told me. I was there.

. . .

March 1931

One evening I'd gone with friends to the Landmark Tavern, a
speakeasy in Hell's Kitchen, a tough part of Queens. My parents
were immigrants—my dad German and my mom Irish—and
both had died in the Spanish Influenza epidemic when I was nine.
I was sent to live with the nuns, and my much younger siblings
went to live with an aunt. On my eighteenth birthday I'd gotten
my inheritance. It was a fine chunk of change for a young girl
and I left the convent, nine years being enough for anyone, and

set myself up in a decent apartment on W 72nd Street. I'd done a lot of writing in my time with the sisters and decided I'd be a freelancer. In two years, I'd managed to get a few bylines in the entertainment pages of *The Evening World* and *The Tribune,* and I wanted to work up a piece on jazz for *The New Yorker.* I'd already pitched it to an editor there, and she was willing to at least have a look. I was on a mission to go to as many jazz clubs as possible, which in 1931 meant going to as many speakeasies as possible.

My friend Russ knocked a secret knock on the heavy Dutch door at the bottom of a steep, dim stairwell behind an Italian restaurant. The door cracked open, Russ said, "Marvin sent me," and we were ushered in. The air was blue with smoke and the sharp tang of bootleg gin, and we squeezed into the last empty table, close to the stage in back. A waitress took our order, while on stage, a combo made up of clarinet, cornet, drums, piano and saxophone started their set. Then someone yelled, "Raid!"

"Jesus, no!" my friend Millie screamed and, in her rush to get up, spilled her gin-tonic all over my new geometric print silk dress. People scrambled blindly, knocked over chairs and tables, trying to make it out before the cops burst in.

Someone grabbed my arm. The man, blond and round-faced, in a tattered, rumpled suit, held a cornet in one hand. "Come on. This way. We'll never make it out the doors."

He was right. The roiling crowd jammed the stairs and the police banged on the door, demanding to be let in. I dodged with him into a dim hallway behind the stage. He pulled me into a janitor's closet, closed the door and we crouched in the dark together among brooms, mops and pails.

"Thank you," I said. "I don't—"

He hushed me. "Shh…they might find us," he whispered.

We heard yelling, screaming, feet on the floor, a policeman barking orders through a megaphone. My stomach knotted as the sound of footfalls approached in the hallway.

"Flanagan! I need you over here!" someone bellowed, then we heard Flanagan run toward the voice.

We huddled in the dark, dank closet, in the acrid smell of lye soap, ammonia and floor wax for maybe a half-hour, until the noise died down. Then we crept into the hallway and peeked into the silent barroom. Upended tables and chairs lay among shards of glass on the floor. And everyone was gone, no doubt riding in paddy wagons.

"I think we're all right," said the cornet player. "But we should get out of here."

We climbed the stairs and ducked out the back door into the empty alley. "Say, young lady," he said. "You smell of gin."

"No offense, but so do you."

He laughed and produced a rumpled pack of Chesterfields from his jacket pocket. "Cigarette?"

"Sure. Now that we're at liberty to talk, let me introduce myself. I'm Alice. Alice Weiss."

"I'm Bix."

"Bix?" I looked at him, looked at the cornet. "Bix Beiderbecke?"

It was hard to tell in the dim, but I think he might have blushed a little. "That's me."

"I have some of your records at home!"

"I hope you like them."

"Are you kidding? They're swell. Imagine, I've been hiding out in a broom closet with Bix Beiderbecke."

"That's nothing, kiddo. I've been hiding out in a broom closet with a redheaded baby."

We hit it off right away, me and Bix.

. . .

Bix hadn't been in town long when we met. And in spite of his musical reputation, didn't have a steady job. He'd managed to pick up a few gigs at colleges, two with the Dorsey Brothers, another with Benny Goodman and the Dorsey Brothers. Before that show, as we waited for Bix to arrive, I talked backstage with Benny Goodman as he replaced a reed in his clarinet.

"Bix is one of those musicians who hates the limelight, who isn't a performer," he said, taking the reed out of a glass of water and trimming it with his pocketknife. "Yet his talent takes him right into the limelight, whether he likes it or not."

"It's a struggle for him," I said.

Goodman inserted the clarinet mouthpiece back into the body. He peered over his glasses at me and shook his head. "A constant struggle. He told me once that he knew that sooner or later he would be found out as a no-talent phony. It's sad. How do you get someone to believe in themselves?"

"I wish I knew."

I wondered if Bix had a hard time believing in himself because of his parents' disapproval. They wanted him to follow in his father and grandfather's footsteps: become a businessman or a banker, something respectable. In their eyes, there was nothing less respectable than a jazz musician, but it was clear Bix was a musician from the start. One of the clippings in the envelope his sister had sent was from the *Davenport Daily Democrat*, talked about his ability to pick out tunes on the piano by ear when he wasn't even three years old. "Little Bickie Beiderbecke plays any selection he hears!" Ironically, this ability kept him from learning to read music well since he didn't need to. In fact, he wasn't allowed to join the musicians' union in Davenport for this reason. Nonetheless he managed to get in his own way.

Listening to his records now, I notice that no matter who he's playing with, he's always the standout. The way he could riff on a simple melody, slide in and out and around the backbeat, rhythm king. He sounded like he was born playing jazz, not what you might expect from a German-American banker's son. But. Oh, Miss Hannah, there were no oopmas from this corn-fed Iowa boy, just slick syncopation and an angel's sublime sense of melody. I thought that if only I could get him to stop drinking, maybe I could save this angel player from his demons. But now I wonder whether jazz was Bix's purgatorio, and death might have been his release into musical perfection. I guess I'll never know.

Though self-taught Bix wouldn't have said so himself, he was a musician's musician. I remember walking around Central Park with him on a warm Sunday afternoon, when he was sober (or so I thought), before he got sick. He told me with a little pride, "Hoagy Carmichael told me he almost fell onto a desk the first time he heard me play."

"Poor Hoagy. Sounds like he might have had a few too many."

"Very funny. And then there was that time Louis Armstrong came to jam with me and some of the boys and ended up in tears."

"What? What awful things did you fellas say to him?"

"Nothing! He said it was because he realized he could never play cornet as good as me."

"Well. What's all this telling you, Bix? Is the message getting through?"

We found a bench under the cool shade of a huge oak tree, away from the heat and the crowds. "I don't know," he finally said. "I guess some people think I'm pretty good."

"A lot of people," I said, as he pulled me closer and kissed me.

· · ·

After Bix died, I read that the composer Maurice Ravel had dropped into a recording session of Bix's in 1928, joined the group for a few numbers, and was extremely impressed with Bix's playing. Bix loved Stravinsky, Schoenberg, and Debussy and was himself a pianist and composer as well as a cornet player. He made recordings of three of his own piano works: "In a Mist," "Candlelights," and "Flashes." What would he have gone on to do, how much more music would he have created if he'd had the chance?

But he didn't get the chance. His drinking was out to get him. Drinking had got him expelled from the private school his parents enrolled him in—the lure of nearby Chicago jazz clubs was too much temptation for him. Then drinking got him expelled from the University of Iowa. He spent much of his life touring with different bands—the Wolverines and Jean Goldkette's Orchestra among others. A star player on four number-one records in 1928 with the Paul Whiteman Orchestra, he had a breakdown while on a road trip with the band, caused by delirium tremens, the D.T.s. Exhausted, he returned to the family home in Davenport to rest the summer before we met. He might have stayed in Davenport longer, but he made a discovery one day that made him decide to leave.

"I was looking for some shoe polish in my parents' upstairs linen closet," he told me one night after we'd had spaghetti for dinner at my apartment. "And I came across a wooden crate. It was full of all the records—my records—that I'd been sending back home to Mom and Pop over the years."

He paused, his lips a grim, straight line, drew a flask from his shirt pocket and offered it to me. I shook my head, thought about how he said he'd quit, but bit my tongue. This was not the time for a lecture. He took a swig and finally I said, "That's awful."

He sighed, his hands trembling, his face flushed. "They never even opened them. They were still in the envelopes I sent them in. I put the lid back on the box and put it back where I found it. Right then I decided to move to New York."

"Aw, Bix. That must have hurt."

"Yes. Yes, it did."

I scrambled for what to say to make him feel better. Maybe there wasn't anything that could make you feel better when you own Mom and Pop treated you like that. "Look at it this way.

Maybe if that hadn't happened, you would never have come to New York. You wouldn't have got the gig playing in that speakeasy where we got to hide in the closet together."

He smiled. "You're right, kid. The night we met turned out to the luckiest night of my life so far."

"The best is yet to come, for both of us. I'm sure of that."

He cleared his throat. "I'm glad you think so, Alice. I'd love to marry you, but I just can't do it until I have a couple thousand in the bank."

I showed him my bankbook, winked and said, "You've got it."

Still, my having money in the bank wasn't good enough for him. We got engaged in June. He quit drinking for good this time, he said, and after that he took on as many gigs as he could. As long as it was a paying gig, he would play anywhere, anytime, with anyone, until any crazy hour. The heat in New York got to him and late-night work was wearing him out. Before long, he caught a bad cold. It rapidly took a turn for the worse and became pneumonia.

. . .

August 1931

On the afternoon of August 6th, I visited Bix in his sweltering apartment on 46th St., a few blocks from mine. He didn't eat much of the sandwich I'd made him, and his coughing was worse than ever. But he felt well enough to play piano for almost an hour. Even sick, his playing was rapturous, a refinement of romantic rag stride, a combination of Debussy and the Duke. Around seven, I could see he was getting tired. He got into bed and I turned off the lights and kissed him.

"When are your mom and brother arriving?"

"In a couple of days. I'll be fine by the time they get here, wait and see."

"Sure, you will. Goodnight, Bix."

"Goodnight, kiddo. Come back tomorrow, will you?"

"I will. Sleep tight, my love."

. . .

A couple of hours later, right after Rudy Vallee's radio show, a knock came on my door.

"Miss Alice Weiss?" asked the grim-faced officer. "I'm afraid I have some bad news about your fiancé, Mr. Beiderbecke."

He took me back to Bix's apartment, and there he was, as quiet and still as when I'd left him but on a stretcher. I fell to my knees and wept over his body, his lips already turning cold in the heat of the summer night.

Then they took him away. When I had calmed down a little, the building manager told me he'd heard screams coming from Bix's apartment around 9:30. Bix had answered his knock, trembling violently, pointing to his bed.

"He said two Mexicans with long daggers were hiding under it. I got down and looked, to make him feel better. And then he just fell. I ran across the hall to get the doctor who lives there but it was already too late. I'm sorry."

Soon the same policeman took me back to my apartment. I cried long into the night.

I met Mrs. Beiderbecke and Bix's brother, Burnie, briefly before they returned home, I decided not to go to Davenport with them for the funeral. How could I face all those people I didn't know, the rest of Bix's family and friends and neighbours, in Iowa? Lord knew it wouldn't matter to Bix anymore.

. . .

January 1955

Bix was twenty-eight when he died. I was twenty-one. "I'll change him," I thought when we met. Now, of course, I know how naïve that expectation of youth was.

Maybe alcohol would have killed him sooner or later anyway, but I can't help thinking about the unregulated, black market, poisonous hooch that so many people drank during Prohibition. Bix wasn't the only one to be poisoned, not the only to die so young because of it. How many hearts broken, how many lives torn apart? There's probably no way to know.

Bix didn't want to be a public person, like I said before, and I respected that, then and now. I've often thought about writing a book, setting the record straight once and for all about the details of his life. What always stops me is knowing that he wouldn't want me to.

I finish my coffee, carry Bix's records back downstairs, close the crate carefully, and put it back in its place on the shelf. I hope he knows that his records are not unplayed—I've listened to them all over these years. I love him still.

THIS IS A TEST

Mariah Dufty got a framed picture off her dresser, a family portrait. Her mom and Duane stood behind blonde little Mariah, who smiled broadly with her eyes closed. Her older sisters stood beside her. They wore church clothes, Easter clothes maybe, out on their front lawn. Diana and Michelle both had long straight hair, Diana glared from kohl-ringed eyes. They looked like the sullen girls from the junior high we saw at the bus stop across from our school, who'd chew gum and smoke and thankfully didn't even notice us when we walked by.

"My dad died when I was little," she said. "I don't remember him much. My sisters look like him, kind of dark. Duane's been around about as long as I can remember. Michelle says too long. I was in kindergarten when that picture was taken. That would make Michelle just about my age now, and Diana would have been in grade eight."

"They must be done school, now, right?"

"They were done with school a long time ago. Neither of them actually finished. Diana moved out when she was sixteen. She lives in Edmonton now with her boyfriend. And Michelle ran away when she was fourteen. Last we heard she was in Vancouver. Mom's kind of worried. Duane says she should get over it, Michelle just does it for attention."

I nodded, tried to think of a response.

"I know where Michelle is," she added quietly. "I call her sometimes, collect, when Mom and Duane are out. I have her number memorized so I'll never have to write it down. She keeps telling me to get out now before it's too late. I can come and live with her, she says. Look what happened to Diana, she says."

Mrs. Keller opened the bedroom door just then. "Donna? Mariah? Come into the kitchen for some lemon bars."

What did happen to Diana, I wondered as we went down the hall into the kitchen.

. . .

"There's a ghost in the Dufty's backyard. You've got to run every time you go by their place," Kelly Burke told me on the way to school a couple of weeks earlier.

I didn't know Kelly all that well yet, didn't know anybody all that well yet since my family had only been in town about a month. She'd seemed all right, as did Tina Kozma and Patty Exner, the other girls I sat with in Mr. Stevens' class. Perhaps it was another new-kid dupe. There'd been a few of them so far, tests to see what I was made of, how quick I was on my feet. Like the one big moon-faced Oliver Richter had conducted on me. He'd walked up to me at recess once and declared that he hated all people from Saskatchewan. "So do I," I told him. He backed off, a frown creasing the broad expanse of his forehead. Well, if you can't beat 'em, confuse 'em.

I looked across the street at the square bungalow Kelly nodded at, turquoise with peeling white trim, flowerbed full of red and purple tulips in need of deadheading, orange poppies and brilliant white phlox that spilled onto the overgrown lawn. And it was true, as kids neared the yard, they'd break into a run and slow again at the alley.

"Dufty? Like Mariah Dufty?"

Kelly nodded. "That's her. She's got two older sisters, too, but they don't go to St. Dymphna anymore. Haven't you noticed how weird she is?"

Now there was a question. If I said yes, she'd ask why I talked to Mariah. If I said no, I'd be branded as an idiot. That Mariah was weird was the first thing you'd notice about her, pretty much the first thing you'd notice about our class. Our desks were all arranged in groups, but Mariah's sat off by itself, a heap of half-read books and elaborate drawings that Mr. Stevens was always after her to clean up. She read and drew and dreamed over in her corner, seemed unaware of what went on around her. Her long, pale hair hung around her long, pale face; her eyes, lightest of green, fringed with white brows and lashes, almost faded into it. She was all one colour except for her clothes, and you knew the person who planted the flowers out front of their house made her clothes, too, like the orange and green plaid jumper she'd wear over a mauve nylon turtleneck.

"C'mon, Kelly. A ghost?"

"Really. You want to be staying away from there, believe me."

Clearly, Kelly was warning me. But was she trying to help me, or giving me a dare?

. . .

I finally agreed, after Mariah asked a few times, to come over one Friday after school. Her excitement was almost painful to watch. Was there something special I'd like for a snack, she wanted to know? She'd get her mother to make it. If it was nice out, maybe she could show me her garden. If it wasn't, she had some books and drawings she wanted to show me, some records we could listen to. I started to wish I'd never accepted her invitation, wished I'd kept making excuses. I could have said I had to help my mother, I had an appointment, we were going out for dinner that night, anything. This constant nattering about my visit was getting to be too much, like nobody'd ever visited before.

Now that her courage was up, she started to just come up and talk to me out of the blue. Already I could see it wasn't doing me any good socially. One morning as we lined up to go to gym, she asked if I liked coconut macaroons or date squares better. I looked over her shoulder at Kelly watching us. Thankfully, Kelly was far enough away that she couldn't hear us. I mean, I couldn't let anyone know about this.

When Friday came, I felt a little sick all day, thinking about after school. I'd considered feigning illness and missing school that day but decided it would be best to get it over with. Mariah wouldn't be put off for long, I was sure. We'd reschedule and reschedule until I'd eventually have to tell her I didn't want to come over, I'd have to tell her to leave me alone. And I couldn't do it, I wouldn't. I'd go to her house, I wanted to see her drawings, maybe I even wanted to be her friend. Only why did she have to make it so hard? Couldn't she see I was doing this at grave personal risk to myself, couldn't she just be quiet about it?

The one good thing about Mariah's constant and extreme pokiness was that by the time she got it together at the end of the day and we started off to her house, everybody else had long gone. I told her that I absolutely had to be home by 5:00. It gave me some strange consolation to think that every second she poked around meant a second off my visit.

We came into the house through the side door and went up three stairs into the kitchen. The counters were covered with stacks of Jell-O packages. Mrs. Dufty stood with her back to us, cooking something. She had the radio on and didn't hear us come in. When she opened a cupboard, I saw more Jell-O boxes crammed in every available space, as if she had it on good authority that they were going to stop making it, and then where would she get the gelatinous goodness her family loved?

"Hello, Mrs. Dufty," I said, and she turned around. Mariah's mom looked much like her; pale and long-faced, though her colourless hair was cut into a practical pixie cut. She wore a purple, brown and green mottled pattern dress which had the unfortunate effect of accentuating the large bruise on her thin arm just above the elbow.

"Oh, it's not Mrs. Dufty anymore," Mariah cut in. "It's Mrs. Keller, now. She and Duane got married last year. And I got to be the flower girl, right, Mom?"

"I wish you'd call him Dad, not Duane. Now why don't you girls go and play quietly? He'll be home soon, and you know he needs quiet when he gets home, and I have too much to do before he gets here."

As we started down the hall to Mariah's room, I could see what her mom meant about having things to do. Like putting all that food away. More Jell-O and other packaged foods were stacked on the dining room table, stacked up on the floor against the walls in the hallway. Tapioca pudding, gravy browning, canned soups. Mariah didn't say anything about them, and I didn't ask.

Mariah must have had hundreds of her own artworks on her bedroom walls. And maybe thousands piled on the floor, stacked in the closet. Paintings, drawings in pencil, charcoal, pastel, pen and ink. Pictures of horses, winged and ordinary, dragons, unicorns, chimera, castles, knights and ladies. As she explained all about the subjects and the materials she used, I noticed something about her that I'd noticed before. When she talked about her pictures, she was animated, lit up. She was no longer pale, but luminous. She spoke with her whole body, gestured, paced up and down the room. Like she was letting me in on the experience she was having because she knew I understood.

And I'd seen her have that experience before, I knew now. Silently, by herself, at school when she drew. She put everything into her work, became completely absorbed by it, the same quiet glow shining from her eyes. When she drew, she was where she wanted to be, needed to be, and she was lucky she knew how to get there. Some people spend their whole lives trying to get there and never find it.

Later, we sat at the yellow formica kitchen table eating lemon bars and drinking milk. The sulphur smell of whatever Mrs. Keller was cooking, cabbage maybe, took the edge off my appetite. Or maybe it was thinking about what had happened to Mariah's sister. Part of me wanted to know, part of me didn't. I tried to listen to Mariah saying we should walk over to the public library together sometime. But I kept wondering about Diana, picking at my lemon bar, which tasted not at all of lemon, just bland and sweet, and stealing glances at the bruise on Mrs. Keller's arm. I could see now it was in the shape of fingers.

· · ·

At ten to five I told Mariah I had to leave soon. I got up to leave and she gave me a guided tour of the knickknacks on the shelves that lined the front hallway. She didn't want me to go. But now we were only a couple of feet from the open front door and the gentle scent of flowers blew in on the warm breeze through the screen door.

Through the living room window, I saw a rusted brown truck pull into the driveway. I didn't want to be there when Duane got in. Mariah still nattered, though I wasn't really listening anymore, and I scrambled to gather up my books and tie my shoes. I heard the back door open, heard work boots going up the stairs into the kitchen. The radio snapped off.

This would be my last chance to ask about Diana. "What so what *did* happen to your sister?" I whispered.

"She had to have an operation," Mariah whispered back.

"What kind of operation?"

"A baby operation."

"What? What kind of—"

"Shh. He'll hear you. I gotta go now, Donna. Bye," she said, nudging me out the front door and closing it behind me.

. . .

I didn't realize I was running until I almost crashed into Kelly. "What were you doing in Mariah Dufty's house?" Her freckled nose crinkled up like she smelled something unpleasant.

"Visiting."

"You went to hang out at Mariah Dufty's after school?"

"Yeah."

"You're kidding. What was it like?"

"What do you mean what was it like? It was like anybody else's house." This was not really true, not at all, but I wouldn't give Kelly the satisfaction.

"What about the ghost?"

"What about it? You don't really believe that, do you?"

"Sure I do. You should, too."

. . .

After that, I knew the end was near. It happened pretty fast after the Scotch tape incident. I brought my own tape to school, and it didn't take long for Kelly, Tina and Patty to start borrowing tape from me. Pretty soon I was going through a roll a week. Then Mom said I'd have to buy it myself. I didn't mind sharing a little tape now and then, but I was not prepared to continue providing these girls with tape paid for out of my allowance. Especially since they didn't use it to tape, say, torn pages in books or something. No, they used it to tape pictures of the Bay City Rollers onto their binders, they used it to tape little rainbows they'd drawn onto their pencils, they used it, I finally realized, just to use it up. Another test.

Mr. Stevens had declared an all-day drama class, as he often did on Fridays. Participation was optional, so while most of the class once again acted out Jesus Christ Superstar along to the record, our group sat at our desks. I was drawing, as I did whenever I could.

"Donna, I need tape," said Tina, not even looking at me, centering Shaun Cassidy on the front of a notebook.

"I'm out."

"What?"

"I'm out. You guys used it all up, and I'm not bringing any more. Get your own tape," I said.

Patty stopped chewing the ends of her hair. "Listen to this girl. Bring our own tape?"

"Next thing you know she'll be moving her desk over there, with Mariah."

It wasn't exactly that I'd been avoiding Mariah since the visit. Well, I had been, but not completely. It was just that I had come to know for certain that that my choices were either remain in the mid-to-low level popularity group with Kelly, Tina and Patty, or join Mariah as an outcast. I could not have both.

Mariah heard her name and looked up from her book for a second. I panicked, could not make eye contact, looked instead for some lost article in my desk. How could I choose, why should I have to?

The lunch bell rang, and everyone else left. Kelly turned around and asked if I was coming. "In a minute," I told her.

"Girls," said Mr. Stevens. "It's time to go." He turned the lights off and left. Mariah sat there alone in the dim classroom, and I wondered what went through her mind that she could just ignore the whole world like that.

"I'm going home for lunch, Mariah. Are you going to read that book the whole noon hour?"

"I brought my lunch. I'm going down to the gym to eat when I'm done this chapter."

"Okay. Well, I'll see you later."

. . .

No one in our group was too surprised when I hauled my desk to the other side of the room after lunch. Patty snorted though her nose, Tina told me to have fun. Kelly looked a little hurt, I think, or maybe concerned. It was hard to tell. The green rubber desk feet squeaked and ground on the floor as I dragged it over, and it seemed to me that everyone was watching.

The view was different on Mariah's side of the room. I knew I'd like being able to see out the window. Mariah took great pleasure in turning her desk around so I'd be able to see the board, in clearing away some of the detritus, in making room. Then she dug around in her desk, searching for something, and finally produced a roll of tape.

A GOOD LONG LIFE

A row of black birds sat on the clothesline on an October morning as I lingered over the paper at the kitchen table after breakfast. Soon, not having to rush off to work in the mornings would be the new normal for me. I had no idea yet that when the baby came, while I might not be going to work, lingering in peace over the newspaper would be a thing of the past for a long while. I put the paper in the recycling bin and looked more closely at the birds: they were actually socks. Ten black socks, covered in frost, hanging on the line.

They hadn't been there the night before, and they weren't my socks, or Mike's. I felt the baby flutter and fought back nervousness, apprehension. Someone had come and hung socks on our clothesline sometime in the night. I wondered if I should take them down and show this weird person they couldn't just be going around hanging things on our clothesline. But then, I didn't like the idea of touching them.

I put the dishes in the dishwasher, thought about calling Mike at work. And then I saw a thin man with wispy white hair taking the socks off of the line, moving slowly. Mr. Petrovich, the man we'd bought the house from in the summer. I stepped out the back door.

"Mr. Petrovich."

He didn't hear me at first, so I called again a little louder. The second time he squinted over in the direction of my voice. As I got closer to him, he recognized me.

"Good morning, Jenn," he said. "I hope you don't mind I am coming back to hang my socks. At my apartment, there is nowhere for hanging washing."

By this time, I knew there was no point in asking Mr. Petrovich any of the many questions that sprang into my mind right then, such as: *You wash only your socks? You can't hang them in your bathroom somewhere? You drove for fifteen minutes last night to get here and hang them up, and then fifteen minutes to come back here this morning to get them? You drove, period?* Mr. Petrovich, a widow for ten years, was ninety-five years old, and at his children's insistence had sold the family home, where he'd lived for forty-five years, and moved into an assisted living residence.

A couple of weeks after we took possession in August, he'd shown up on the step looking for the toilet brush he'd left behind. When I'd come across the brush, at least forty years old, with a cracked black-and-gold sparkle plastic handle and worn-down bristles, I tossed it without a second thought.

"You threw it away?"

"It was dirty."

"It was a good brush." He'd looked genuinely hurt, and baffled that I would throw away what he saw as a perfectly good and functional tool.

He put the last of his socks into a plastic Co-Op bag and nodded toward the garden. "Are you digging the potatoes yet?"

"Um, no. Not yet."

I had dug up a few of the crop of small, scabby potatoes in our massive new garden and doubted it was worth my time to harvest the rest of them, along with the beets and carrots and dill that had been planted in the Petrovich garden every year since 1952. And I knew I wouldn't have time or energy to pick many more of the small green apples from the five trees in the backyard before the frost took them.

We'd got the house for a song because it was a fixer-upper, but much bigger than our previous house and in a better location. When we viewed it, it was crammed to the rafters with stuff, and the family assured our real estate agent that it would all be cleaned out before we moved in. That never happened; we should have got that assurance in the contract, not just verbally. Mr. Petrovich was left to clear the forty-five-year accumulation by himself, and he wasn't up to the huge task. Apparently one of his daughters, middle-aged and unwell herself, had come to town for a weekend to help. The other children, our agent said, were estranged from Mr. Petrovich to varying degrees and would not help. Between unpacking from our move and getting rid of the endless piles of junk in the house and garage—decades-old spices and canned goods; shelves groaning with murky jars of preserves that Mrs. Petrovich had put up before she died; frozen apples, potatoes and beets from God only knew when; old sour cream containers full of rusted-together bolts; salvaged pieces of wire; a lifetime's worth of plastic bread bag closers—I was exhausted. Not to mention that I was pregnant and working part-time. Yeah, the potatoes were not high on the list right then.

"They're good potatoes. You can leave them in the ground until it snows. They'll keep you going all winter."

"Why don't you take some with you?"

"No. I got nowhere to keep them. And they cook for me where I live now, so it's okay. I should go, I got a doctor's appointment."

He said goodbye and drove off in his powder blue late seventies model Buick that he'd parked behind our back fence. As he pulled away, the lady from across the alley waved me over. A

tiny, elderly Chinese woman, she had no English, but the annoyance in her voice came through. She pointed at Mr. Petrovich's
departing car, covering one eye with her hand, then pointed at
the large dent I'd noticed before on her white aluminum garage
door. She kept talking and repeating the movements and it was
clear that she felt Mr. Petrovich could not see and had backed
into her garage door.

"That's too bad," I murmured, not sure what else to say. Mr.
Petrovich had made an impression on her; I could see that.

. . .

A few mornings later, I found Mr. Petrovich in the back yard
again, although this time there were no socks on the line. He
was slowly but determinedly hoeing the weeds in the garden.

"Mr. Petrovich."

"Good morning. When I was last time here, I noticed the
weeds, so I thought I'd help out."

"You don't need to do that."

"It's okay, I don't mind. If you don't keep on top of the
weeds, they choke everything else out. Even frost doesn't kill
them, you know."

"Mike and I can do this later," I lied. We had no intention
of doing anything about the weeds. We had to get rid of all the
junk he'd left behind before the baby was born. Why didn't he
want to help us with that?

"I know you're busy working," he said. "It's okay."

This is our yard now, I wanted to say. Instead, I sighed and
said, "Are you sure you don't want to take some potatoes home?
We've used up most of the carrots and beets, but we'll never be
able to eat all those potatoes."

He leaned heavily on the upright hoe, blade stuck between
chickweed-covered hills of potato plants, his long, thin blue-
veined hands clutching the handle. "I don't have any place

to keep them. But you can put them in the deep fridge downstairs."

I didn't have the heart to tell him that we'd thrown out all the plastic containers and bags of ancient frozen food that had filled the ancient chest freezer. Or that two eager and strong recent arrivals from Newfoundland had responded to our ad: *Full-size chest freezer, free. Working condition. You must remove.* I couldn't believe they were able to haul the thing up the dark narrow basement stairs and down the back steps.

"I'll see if I have time. Do you want something to drink?"

"I don't think so. I'm a little tired now, but I can come back later and do some more."

"Mr. Petrovich, you don't need to come and weed our garden." Was that enough of a hint?

"I don't mind. But I'll go to my apartment now."

I talked to Mike about it over dinner. He'd spent an hour working on the junk in the garage after work; traces of cobwebs clung to his sandy hair and his blue eyes were rimmed red from the dust.

"I guess he's not hurting anything," Mike said.

"Well, no. But he doesn't seem to get the idea that it's not his house anymore."

"I know, Jenn. But he probably has nothing to do all day. I'm sure he'll stop coming eventually."

"I hope so."

. . .

A thin woman in a light blue cardigan with shoulder-length brown hair stood on the step when I answered the doorbell one day. I wondered for a moment if it was another of the door knockers in this new neighbourhood who perpetually wondered if I had a moment to talk about Our Lord and Saviour (no, I never did).

"I'm Barb Petrovich," she said, extending her hand. "John Petrovich's daughter."

"Would you like to come in?"

She stepped inside. "I'll just be a minute. Dad asked me to bring you these." She handed me a clear plastic bag full of keys.

"Do you know what they're for?"

"Probably mostly for the front door. He would misplace them and then get a new key cut. Some of them might be for the back or the garage. Congratulations, by the way," she said, glancing at my bump. "When are you due?"

"Thanks. I'm due in March. Trying to get organized before then. I was wondering—did you want us to put aside anything that we find?"

"Oh, no. We went through it all after Mom died. I am sorry the place was such a mess."

Is such a mess. Still, I corrected silently. "We're just trying to get it cleared up before the baby comes."

"Of course. Well, I'll leave you to it, then."

Annoyance rose in me after she left. The place was a mess, a hell of a mess. They said they would deal with it, and they didn't. Every time I saw all the junk, or saw Mr. Petrovich poking around in our yard, it added to my frustration, my fear that we wouldn't finish it before the baby came. And I already had enough anxiety about having a baby.

. . .

The kitchen cupboards, the closets, the basement and the garage were all crammed full of junk, more junk than we realized before we bought the house. The garage was the worst, but the basement was a close second. Among the thousands of things we found down there was a box full of cerlox-bound booklets, Mr. Petrovich's memoir, entitled *A Good Long Life*. One of his daughters had typed, photocopied and bound it, as she noted in her introduction. In it, we learned that at age fourteen he'd been press-ganged into the Tsar's army, where an injury blinded his left eye. He left the Ukraine for Canada after the Revolution. The booklet's forty pages covered his migrant farm work across the prairies during the Depression, his settling in Calgary and working in construction, and his family life. He and his wife had raised seven children, one of whom had died of cancer in childhood. The memoir ended at the time of his wife's death.

Odd that they would leave these behind. Would someone in the family not want these? Were they just extras? I would mention them to Mr. Petrovich the next time I saw him.

. . .

We had the windows open on a Sunday afternoon, the first warm spring day after blue-eyed, sandy-haired James was born in March. Our lives, after six weeks, began edging toward normal again. We still hadn't had more than four uninterrupted hours of sleep since James was born. But at least now he was nursing properly—I no longer had to pump milk and bottle-feed it to him, a process which consumed most of my time while it lasted. He was colicky, but his nightly screaming seemed to be gradually diminishing, and other parents we knew assured us that colic didn't last forever; it only seemed that way at the time. I felt like there was hope that things were getting better. Spring was coming. And we would have a good night's sleep again someday, I knew it.

Mike was in the garage, still clearing junk out, and James was down for a nap when the phone rang. I'd forgotten to turn the ringer off as I usually did at nap time, and I leapt for the phone.

It was Barb Petrovich. "I wanted you to know that Dad's in the hospital."

"I'm sorry to hear that."

"Yes. Well, he is almost ninety-six. He has pneumonia, and at that age it can be serious."

"That's too bad. I hope he's better soon."

"I hope so, too. Anyway, I wonder if you might go up and visit him sometime."

"Uh—I suppose we could."

"Great. He's in the Lougheed. And I know he'd like to see you, Jenn. Bring the baby."

Strange that she would ask us to go visit him. We'd bought the house from him—we weren't friends or family. And I couldn't see taking James with to the hospital. But then, I knew he was lonely. Sometime we'd get Mike's mom to babysit and we'd go have a short visit with him.

. . .

We finally had to call in a professional for help with the garage. Although by this time we'd got the house cleaned out, the garage was complicated by the 'root cellar'. Mr. Petrovich had jackhammered a hole in the concrete garage floor and dug out a room that he lined with shelves, which were, surprise, crammed with junk. Or so Mike told me. I didn't ever go down there. We hired a man who came and started pitching stuff into his flatbed truck. Mike gave him a hand, and after a couple of hours they were done. Done. At last, we were rid of all of Mr. Petrovich's junk.

"Look at this," Mike said when he came in. He handed me a small metal sign with two prongs on the bottom, one of those temporary grave markers for before the headstone is ready. The plastic printed tape label read, 'Johnny Petrovich, December 3, 1958–July 14, 1970.'

I read it a couple of times. "He wasn't even twelve," I said.

"I know. And Petrovich held onto it all these years."

"Well. He wasn't exactly good at getting rid of things. And something like that…"

Mike finished for me. "How could you throw it out?"

I handed it back to him. "What are you going to do with it?"

He scratched his head and shrugged. "Throw it out, I guess."

. . .

While reading the paper one morning a few weeks later, I scanned the obituaries as I always do. One heading jumped out at me: *John Petrovich, 1901–1997.* For a moment I thought it was an In-Memoriam notice for Mr. Petrovich's son. The little marker with almost the same name on it flashed in my mind.

'In his ninety-seventh year, John (Ivan) Nikolai Petrovich passed away in hospital after a brief illness,' it began. A long list of children, grandchildren and great-grandchildren followed, none of whom seemed to be around much in his final years. I was ashamed that Mike and I never had got around to visiting him. Still, it sounded like he had lived a good, long life, mostly.

I was about to put the paper in the recycling bin but decided to leave it out so I'd remember to show Mike later. Then James began crying, and I went down the hall to his room.

ACKNOWLEDGMENTS

Huge thanks to Catharina de Bakker and Mel Marginet for believing in these stories and for giving them such a good home. To my editor extraordinaire Lee Kvern—thank you for bringing your wise heart and soul and vision to this book. I am so grateful for all you contributed! To Diane Girard, sincere gratitude for your assistance with many of these stories. Thank you to Betty Jane Hegerat, Barb Howard, and Rea Tarvydas for their kind help with some others. To Jan Markley, Steve Passey, Laura Nicol, and Ali Bryan—thank you for listening while this book came to be.

I am grateful to the Art Gallery of Ontario for bringing me closer to Tom Thomson. Roy MacGregor's books on Thomson were also invaluable in the writing of "Dominion." Ken Emerson's book *Doo-Dah: Stephen Foster and the Rise of American Culture* was a great help in the writing of "No One to Love." As well, I would like to acknowledge the generous support of the Alberta Foundation for the Arts which allowed me to complete this collection.

My thanks to the editors of the following publications, where many of these stories have appeared previously:

"Vermin" in *Joyland*

"Dominion" in *FreeFall*

"A Good Long Life" in *Room*

"Nurse Ingrid" in *The Saturday Evening Post*

"Only Known Photograph of Chopin, 1849" in *Freshwater Pearls: The Alexandra Writers' Centre Society 30th Anniversary Anthology*

"The Unchanging Sea" in *The Antigonish Review*

"The Hardest Part" in *Agnes & True*

"Good Friday, at the Westward" in *The Prairie Journal*

"Ask Your Mom" in *The Danforth Review*

"The Quality of Mercy" in *New Forum*

"Awkward Positions" in *The Bloody Key Society Periodical*

"No One to Love" in *The Copperfield Review*

"Glory B" in *The Black Dog Review*

"Love Story" in *Bareback Lit*

"Del" in *The Manawaker Studios Fiction Podcast*

An earlier version of "In a Mist" in *Historical Feathers*

An earlier version of "This is a Test" in *The Menda City Review*